COMPLEXES
By C. M. Chua

First Printing, 2014

ISBN 978-0-9908509-1-5

For more information, visit:
www.cmchua.com

Editing by: Caroline Duffy
Cover Design by: Marialaina Nissenbaum

To my support group,
Mom, Roberta, Neville,
For helping me save myself.

Acknowledgements

Even when I was halfway done with *Complexes,* I hardly imagined that I would reach this point, this stunning peak. I asked for a lot of help. I received much more than I anticipated.

While writing, I considered floor E to be a bizarre family. After writing, I found family through the unlikely: Kickstarter. Salome Hanes, Steph Harkavy, Renato Maceda, the Onday family, Jose Viana, Kim Coombs, Aaron Bogdanovsky, Tom Comiskey, Tita Bing, Patty Kirk, and Father Greg – thank you very specially. I also send my love to Mommy Manay, Amber Mazza, Amanda Blanco, Marilou Castro, and Oscar Montalvo, Jr, and Dad. Thank you for supporting me. Thank you for helping me achieve my dream.

I give special thanks to my teachers. They have taught me how to read and write and have always encouraged me to touch the clouds. Mrs. Schaefer, Mrs. Muscolino, Ms. Larson, and Dr. Motto. My years of bothering you with my writing are not quite over.

My friends from Mother Seton deserve a paragraph to themselves. Thank you to Bridget Duffy, for always telling me to follow my dreams. Thank you to Lauren Sauer, for helping me through tough times and for being an excellent sounding board for ideas. Thank you to Marialaina Nissenbaum, for taking the time out of your busy schedule to shoot and design the gorgeous cover photo.

I want to acknowledge The Coffee House in Edison for allowing us to shoot for the cover there. Also, thank you to Kearra Amaya Gopee, for stepping up and taking my headshot.

I also extend special thanks to Caroline Duffy. Without her, *Complexes* would be an unedited mess. She has truly done a wonderful job cleaning up the novel; I really could not have done it without her.

Thank you, Mom. Thanks for letting me rant about the book over the dinner table. Thanks for reading it and giving me earnest feedback. Thanks for keeping me sane throughout this whole process. I really couldn't have asked for a better mother.

Before dramatic music plays to cut me off, I'll insert a tiny shout-out to Neville the cat, my sunshine.

Complexes would be nothing without all of you.

Table of Contents

COMPLEXES

Chapter One

The floors were lettered rather than numbered. Folks guessed that the landlord Miriam Bickel and her ancestors made it so. In truth, no one, including Miriam Bickel and her ancestors, knew why the floors were lettered rather than numbered. Like many of life's mysteries, it remained an unromantic fact to those living in the Complexes.

To Antony Shepherd and many of the Complexes' inhabitants, the lettered floors were neither a blessing nor a curse, but a quirky addition to life in the dreary, gray, cold city. He chortled at the letter E stickered onto the elevator button. Little idiosyncrasies like that always made him want to call the place home. But, even on his first day in the city, in the Complexes, he knew it would not be his home.

Antony and Gerard Shepherd were vagrants. The latter herded his son around the continent, beginning in smelly Frisco apartments and somehow ending on the East Coast. Antony didn't mind, or at least, he'd convinced himself, just as he'd convinced himself of his mother's early death, of that much. The lack of home and heritage bothered him as much as the hum of an air conditioner on a hot day—at first invasive, then almost soothing, then background noise.

But in today's weather, air conditioners and their white noise were

1

CHAPTER ONE

obsolete. It had been so for seven years, and would remain that way for the next three months. Summer had ceased to exist. The cold-blooded world was suffering from a draft.

Antony despised the cold for a very simple reason. If he possessed any worldly renown and was listed as an option in a poll featured in a teenage girl's magazine, he would be a top choice for a "perfect summer fling." Unfortunately, Antony didn't relish "flings" much. Doubly unfortunate, the biting climate gnawed away at his natural West Coast tan and froze his ocean eyes. His blond hair, like flowers, wilted. Any cell of inherited attractiveness gathered in clusters of flushed red, when he'd hold his steaming tea to his nose, buried his hands in just-dried clothes, or stared at any lady long enough to force his ears to turn the kind of red that blooms from under your skin.

His father was just the same. Antony was fully aware of this and couldn't help but notice his glowing ears when a woman greeted them as they lugged their boxes and bags into E11.

"This must seem suburban of me, but welcome. The heating is in Marie's room right now, so you'll have to endure with the rest of us."

"Ah, thanks—I'm Gerard, and—what's your name, Miss …?"

"Mrs. Speare. Mara."

COMPLEXES

Gerard was slightly disappointed by the ring on her finger and the extra syllable slapped onto the obligatory "miss."

She looked beautiful, in a way you'd call exotic if she hadn't appeared so disappointingly domesticated. Something like a retired circus elephant, except the circus hadn't been as theatrical as it was taxing. Her dark olive skin, angular face, and long lashes demanded the addition of a typically advertised Indian accent, but Mara spoke in slow vowels and perfectly attentive consonants. She had an equally slow smile, and attentive eyes.

One look at Gerard's ears would normally raise Antony's own body temperature out of sympathy. However, Antony had eyes for the plate of soft-centered chocolate chip cookies she delicately held as a peace offering. He pinched a particularly steamy one, cupped his other hand around it to prevent the squishy dough from crumbling, and promptly inhaled it as if he were starved.

Gerard lightly bumped the back of his son's head, a punitive habit from years ago that struggled in vain to disappear. "His name's Antony. I'm sorry he's so rude."

"It's okay; they're better freshly baked, right?"

Antony swallowed. "Definitely." He very happily seized the plate of the cookies from her extended proffering.

With emptied hands, Mara seemed to find no other reason to remain at their door.

CHAPTER ONE

"You two can come by anytime, at E01." She waved, closed-fingered, and slid away as fleetingly as she'd arrived. Gerard stared at the faint disturbance of air she left behind, as if her form remained imprinted there like it does on especially soft mattresses or on newly fallen snow.

"Why did you have to be so rude, son?" he complained later. After taking five grand minutes to settle, he'd had plenty of time to replay that fateful encounter, and even more time to ponder the "what-ifs."

"Because she had cookies, the kind that melted in the middle. Anyway, do we have any dinner?"

"I thought I taught you not to take candy from strangers."

"Cookies are different. And if you stared at her like that any longer, she would have left—plate and all." Antony unpacked his few but important belongings. If he judged solely on the starstruck expression glued on his father's face, he figured they'd stay for a while.

Unpacking consumed half an hour, after which Antony found himself listless. Due to the weather, his days would be spent in between walls and floors and ceilings, searching for degrees of comfort, occupation, and heat. "This northeastern climate is *torture* on me," he mused and often whined aloud, because no amount of it would change his father's mind, and it was a scientific fact that it lowers blood pressure. In what he remembered and what was physically impossible to remember, Antony knew he and his father were born to be in the sun. Why they continued to lodge in the world's grayer parts, he couldn't fathom.

It was very gray in this city. There was gray in the cracks of the walls, in the tint of the sky, and in the irises of Mara Speare's eyes. Color and contrast, like heat, were endangered. Only in Antony's dreams, during the fastest REM periods, did he recall the brightness of the world that once was. Whenever he awoke from those dreams and rubbed his eyes with his hands, he'd look at his palms and wonder when they had gotten so gray.

Gerard Shepherd had stumbled upon a Muhammad-ian guardian angel, a bodhisattva, a miracle, a something—and he wasn't going to let it go. The woman with the homemade cookies (little did he know they were really one of those sheets you cut up and stick in the oven) was beautiful in the very essence of beauty.

That was the extent of his verbalization; he was a man of actions rather than words. Gerard would rather shoot first and then ask questions, thereby turning his victim's meaningful final words into gasped disclosures. One can imagine the number of mental mortalities bloodying this man's hands.

One such incident resulted in an unwanted son. At a Haight-Ashbury street fair, he met a crafty woman with hair like sun extensions and an ivory grin as wide as a valley. Gerard loved this solar child with his whole seventeen-year-old being: from the dirt crusted under his toenails to the soft air he'd breathe onto her cheek. Her strangely mature obsession with the juxtaposition of peace, freedom, hemp, and tie-dye drew him into a fatal, six-month-long bear hug that climaxed in nightly tangles of human limbs and bedsheets.

The first time they had sex, Gerard was too frightened to tell her he loved her. The last time they had sex, he figured he'd tell her the next time. But before he'd ever combine guts with heart and become a lover in earnest, he found he had nine months to learn the art of fatherhood first.

When the child came, she had reached her limit of free peace and love. Her farewell consisted of a Post-it on Antony's crib: "I never wanted a child with a man who doesn't love me," it read.

But I do *love her.* He wouldn't have spent those months with her if he didn't, much less accepted his new role as a father. *I love her,* he thought, far too late, and never aloud.

Despite his ignorance to the circumstances of his birth, Antony was painfully aware of Gerard's vacant heart and

COMPLEXES

the natural need to fill anything empty. They hardly remained in one place for more than two years, and for months would live in cheap motels meant for cheap lovers in the cheaper sides of cities. Following something that can only be sensed by a hint in a dream or a spiritual epiphany can either guide you to fabulous places or leave you blindfolded in an already dark world. By the time Gerard hit thirty, they had tacitly submitted to the latter concept with the same prideful mindset that if life was to be spent searching for nothing, they might as well have a damn good time.

In the outskirts of the city, whilst imposing on the hospitality of a rare kind family for the night—Antony, who'd happily inherited his mother's provocative foxiness, was especially pleased to spend the night eyeballing a smoky-eyed girl who resided there—Gerard woke up to a voice mail from his tough-voiced sister, asking if he was in town. Why, yes, we are. Why, yes, we can come hang out for a bit. Why, yes, we are on our way.

This sort of occurrence was called fate, and this moment in particular directed Gerard and Antony to the Complexes, which, in turn, directed them to Mara. At this point, Antony had grown up, the world had grown cold, and Gerard had found exactly what he was searching for—*nothing*, in the deceptive form of desperation and a very pretty face.

By God—how can a little golden wedding ring get in the way?

CHAPTER ONE

"Do I know anything," Ruthy incredulously repeated when asked, "about Mara Speare?"

Five years and a crumbled marriage had certainly creased her up. Her voice, once deep and sultry, now sounded cracked and raspy from years of smoking (*"I've tried to quit, trust me!"*). Gerard had known her since, well, forever; she was the only relative he remained close to, having either disappointed the rest or vanished in all mediums save film photographs. She had uncharacteristically called for a support team as she straightened out her divorce, and thus was the red thread tugging him into the heart of the city.

"First thing I know is that she's off-limits," she said wisely.

"I know she's married."

"That's not what I mean. Marriages are fragile, and a handsome guy like you can easily slip between them. Very easily, in fact." Her face wrinkled further at the touchy subject, but she continued. "Things aren't exactly stable in room E01. They're the kind of people who'll devour you if you extend so much of a helping hangnail."

Ruthy was hardly the happiest color of the rainbow.

"But she's beautiful," he responded rather dumbly, "and if her husband doesn't love her, then he doesn't deserve her."

She snorted. "Don't be a teenage girl. You only know—what? Her name and what her face looks like?"

"I have a feeling about her."

COMPLEXES

Gerard didn't expect a wave of understanding from the Queen of Cynics. He received only a wearied, "Do what you want," and a generous thank-you check to help pay his rent and other pay-me-nots.

Gerard, expecting an extended stay, registered Antony into the nearby school and began job hunting. The bound woman-with-a-band-next-door flitted through his mind constantly, through his subconscious and conscious, as if the concept of her closeness scoffed at the supermarket trivialities he dealt with.

The only tangible traces of Mara Speare that occasionally fluttered like lost, coincidental insects across his path were her two sons, who sometimes ran errands and more often padded across the hallway with a determined knit in their eyebrows, and the wafting scent of the same cookies that had greeted them to the Complexes. Gerard took great interest in the former trace. The younger son, who was a startling haunted pale in comparison to his mother, looked to be around Antony's age. The cold, he knew, would eventually drive his son to remain indoors, so he felt relieved that another boy could entertain Antony's easily bored mind. The elder bore a more striking resemblance to Mara. His narrow eyes, no matter how bottomless, fixated almost obsessively on whatever they happened upon, such that the first time Gerard passed him by, he felt naked under his intrusive stare. Both boys wore an eternally preoccupied aura about them, projecting that they were far too intimidating and completely inapproachable. *What kind of a father,* Gerard often wondered, *would create such frightening children with a sweet-looking mother?*

This father-in-question left for work every morning and arrived home late at night. On his fateful first day at school, Antony had the misfortune to share an elevator with him and his two sons. He relayed the awkward incident to his father, saying crudely, "Standing next to each other, they all look tall and scary as fuck."

In the week that followed, Antony shared his curious observation that the three Speare men never boarded the elevator together again. He did, however, share a class or two with the pale one, although the elephantine discomfort of knowing someone without really *knowing* them prevented him from making friends, or whatever kids call it. Named uniquely as Angus Speare, he was intelligent and haughty, unfriendly, and had an icicle up his ass—in other words, the paragon of the kind of person Antony hated most. Gerard chuckled at the irony.

To say the least, that fortress of a family was impregnable.

"She said we're always welcome, you know," Antony said matter-of-factly.

"It's just a courtesy. Just something people say." Gerard continued with a chortle, "Imagine us marching in there just because we wanted cookie."

COMPLEXES

His face soured and smiled at the same time. "They'd *poison* us."

With a laugh: "True."

Ruthy's E06 had the heating that weekend and Antony fully intended to reap the benefits. His aunt tolerated his presence as a six-year-old tolerates lettuce on the dinner table; his cousin, Morrissey, a preteen with an inherited winning smile and a championship scowl, adored him, and made it her solemn business to know everything about him.

"Are you a virgin?" she deadpanned.

"Why in the world would I tell you that?"

"Are you gay?"

"What?"

"Have you ever kissed a girl?"

Needless to say, her questions were sorely out of order.

No matter how violating, Antony enjoyed her presence. The last time he saw her was when she was seven, and although seven-year-olds were cute and shit, they were no fun when he was preoccupied with more important, twelve-year-old-related thoughts. Fully aware of his power to pervert her at her current, very corruptible age, he decided to be something of a mentor, guiding her to a successful teenage life (the likes of which made him giggle guiltily, as all teenagers tacitly agree that no such thing exists). She'd do anything he told her to, after all.

"Question for a question," Antony proposed. "Why are you asking me this stuff?"

Her blue eyes, quite similar to his, narrowed as she stated the obvious. "You're a boy. An *older* boy."

Mentally, he praised her for her honesty. "Okay, and you wanna know about older boys?"

"*Duh.*"

"Shoot."

Again: "Are you gay?"

He stared down at her triumphantly. "I'm as straight as I want to be."

"How many girls have you dated?"

Antony leaned back, his eyes stretching upward. Being the son of a drifting man, he rarely had the opportunity to engage in the kind of relationship he'd like—with passion, lasting love, romance, corruption via *The Notebook*, et cetera. He did, however, experience bits and pieces of it in quick, determined moments, late-night excursions, basement horror movies, and multiple school dances. His longest romance had lasted half a year, cut short by his father's desire to move. Even then, Antony didn't feel the spark he yearned for. That girl was gone—had been gone for a year. It shocked him how far away and fleeting it seemed now. But he was a dogged one; he wouldn't let it bother him until he turned eighty.

COMPLEXES

"A lot of girls," he answered uncolorfully.

"So you're good with the ladies," she said slyly.

"Come on. I mean, look at me."

Morrissey crossed her arms as she bit down into the juicy meat of the conversation. "How do you get a guy to like you?"

"Depends on the guy."

"Any guy. All guys. I don't have one in particular."

He stared at her disbelievingly. Her expression was unfaltering. "You want to become good with the guys in general? I've got news for you, kid: don't be." She pouted, personally offended by this. "I'm serious!" he half laughed, half implored.

A sitcom answer wasn't what Morrissey was hoping to hear. Edgily, she veered to another subject. "Tell me how to be cool, then."

"Cool? You're joking."

She wasn't. Fed up with him, she marched to her room to do whatever twelve-year-old girls did when they experienced what the kids in New Jersey called "Piscataway Middle School." Antony bemoaned his loss of a companion but didn't follow her. He knew girls. They were like hot tea: they'd cool down eventually into this nice, bearable lukewarm.

Antony, who was a strange hybrid of a social butterfly and a social moth, was quick to become lonely and quicker to fill the gap.

CHAPTER ONE

When his best companion—his father, admittedly—was working for his percent of the rent, and Morrissey was too busy brooding or chatting with friends to pay him any mind, he found a companion in the equally lonely security guard. Sans, a nickname that was presented so matter-of-factly that a real name couldn't be requested, had magnificent sleeve tattoos and an even more magnificent beard that would make Gandalf and Hagrid proud. Despite the temperature, he often mopped his brow with a disgusting yellow handkerchief that looked as though it had cleaned the brows of his forefathers. The huge veins in his arms, poking up like a seam in a shirt, seemed to be drawn by vivid blue permanent pen. His intimidating appearance was, as he told Antony, mostly for his job and secondarily for scaring little children shitless on Halloween. This fact alone was enough to let their friendship grow speedily.

A teenage hideout was made out of Sans's security room on the first floor, decorated with Nirvana posters, makeshift lamps, a hot pink beanie seat, and trip wires feigning as normal computer wires everywhere. What attracted Antony most was the tiny heater sitting on the floor, with which the two warmed their toes. The room was extraordinarily comfortable—after all, Sans was paid to sit in that room and watch folks amble up and down the halls with places to go, people to see. They lived in a relatively calm section of the city, and the only violence originated from drunks and the occasional lost druggie demanding a free joint and a place to crash for the night.

"I got the job from good old Miriam. Nice lady. Hey, shut it! Get past her incredibly large nose and she's actually very nice. We go way back. Not like that, kiddo, not like that. But I know just about everyone that cooped up here once. Interesting people. Interesting people ..."

"So do you know," Antony asked, perking up at this new source of gossip, "about those folks in E01?"

Sans laughed his big *"Ba-ha!"* and boomed, "Them? They're just like everyone else. A little surly, but just like everyone else. Their old man had a good business, then they went bankrupt, and now they're here. They've got their little kinks just like everyone else. Just like everyone else." Antony knew when he was finished talking. Sans tended to repeat little phrases, as if he thought they were funny.

"My dad's infatuated with Mara Speare," Antony confided with a grin. "I'm just curious, you know, help a guy out?"

Sans frowned. "Boy, I'm not a home wrecker. Your daddy's handsome enough to find himself his own woman." He paused, taking interest in a screen on floor E. A suited man, adjusting his tie, left E08, and then walked stiffly out of the building. Something in this further inspired him, and he said lowly,

CHAPTER ONE

"Just wait for that home to wreck itself. It'll wreck itself."

That was hint enough for Antony. He dropped the subject warily, reminded suddenly of his own unknown mother. She was a question he never attempted to clarify; it made his father happy to put it behind him—which was ironic, given they were chasing the coattails of the footprints of whims and rainbow-ends all due to the separation. When Antony was fourteen, he'd debated demanding the truth from Gerard. Once he approached him with full resolve to learn what had happened at his birth, he faltered and never attempted to ask again. The crushed look on his father's face at any slight mention of his mother—or lack thereof—was enough.

Antony eventually assumed his mother had died suddenly. That was that. She was gone, and his father was facing the loss. Even if she wasn't dead, she was dead to him anyway. It wasn't a satisfying answer, but it was something that ended, definitively, with a period and a long page break. He'd convinced himself of this theory simply because the very idea of his mother leaving his father pained him, just as a child would feel at his parents' divorce. Antony, a person who really felt things, was all too susceptible to that pain.

Angus Speare looked like the kind of person who really felt things, too.

Spending multiple days worshipping the feet-heater contraption and watching people walk up and down hallways with as much interest as a housewife would a soap opera gave Antony plenty of opportunity to snatch tidbits of the life of his fellow tenants. More than once he caught Angus doing the laundry with his mother and sharing casual passerby conversation with an Asian teenager whose hair was cropped daringly short. Never was he spotted leisurely strolling with his other two family members—the eldest of which, according to Sans, habitually arrived home during ungodly hours of night or just minutes before sunrise.

The Speare family wasn't the only interesting tenant of the Complexes. A ginger, Cheshire-like student who reeked of art major. Down in E10 lived an obligatory batty old lady who squandered her pocket change on a tea collection that would shame both the English and the Chinese. Of course, there were Sans, the two Shepherd men, the previously mentioned Asian girl and her family, and a woman nicknamed "Roonie." Sans didn't disclose what, exactly, was her deal, but judging from the strange alias, Antony could make an accurate guess. Sans himself claimed to have been born dull in every sense of the word, and simply tolerated his companion's occupational prying.

The bare truth was that Antony loved people. Not that he got lonely easily—no, although that was also true. Years and years of travelling had taught him how to fleetingly deduct human value. He liked crushing facades and raining on monotonous parades.

CHAPTER ONE

Some would call it home wrecking. Antony was much more considerate than that. It was more like ... being-that-nosy-person-who-begins-the-soundtrack-of-your-life's-new-meaning.

He had something of a complex about his strange skills.

"At least you're taking an interest now," Sans commented. "We're going to be stuck with each other once the weather gets worse."

He didn't repeat himself. There wasn't anything funny about it.

"You might as well drink it. It's not like I'm enforcing a coffee tax."

"What is it, then? A consolation present?"

"My God! Can't two guys have a civilized conversation over Starbucks anymore?" If Jonathan hadn't been decidedly well-mannered, he would have resolved to chug Angus's drink for him, scalding or not. He'd recently slipped into the habit of oversleeping, which, ironically enough, exhausted him more than constant all-nighters. Caffeine was his salvation—had been since the tenth grade. How anyone could deny a free cup, he couldn't fathom. Then again, this was Angus he was talking about. Not only Angus, but an angry, angsty Angus. Treating someone to a cup of coffee was the modern-day method of declaring a truce, but

COMPLEXES

Jonathan could see how one-sided this contract might be.

The boy was glaring at him, his stare more scathing than the boiled water. "I don't swing that way," Angus said, embarrassed.

Jonathan was almost offended by this. "Asking someone out to coffee is not exactly equivalent to asking someone out to a date. Besides, you're jailbait and head over heels for—uh, Jessie?" He nodded wisely when Angus extracted his phone from his pocket to answer a text message. "Yes, *Jessie*."

"What about her?" he asked venomously, suddenly on the defensive.

Jonathan jumped on the bandwagon, hoping to get on his good side, or even tilt the balance toward his favor. "She's cute and unique, and I can see you guys potentially clicking. I think she might like you back if you get a little more forward, you know? Girls really like that."

Angus softened at the advice, only slightly. Had he been worldlier, he would have been offended at Jonathan's stab at his ability to attract females. Sheepishly, he said, "But I don't think that's what you wanted to talk to me about."

Now *you want to talk.* He leaned back, embracing the powerful feeling of conversation control. "Nah, unless you want to talk about it."

Angus countered suspiciously, "You obviously have ulterior motives."

CHAPTER ONE

Jonathan cringed at those two words juxtaposed. "Stop making me sound like a pedophile."

"What did you do to my brother?"

That was quick. "I have done"—he could envision the jury leaning forward in their seats, craning their necks in anticipation—"absolutely nothing to him."

"Bullshit," Angus snapped. One would have thought Jonathan had played a queen when Angus had all four in his hand. The kid was fast, and liked control.

"Well, what did Jessie do to you?" The question didn't quite register. Jonathan was getting impatient with blank-faced teenagers in general. "I mean, you meet someone special, and suddenly you're this brand new guy. Angus version one-point-one. It's not like she *did* anything, physically forcing you or warping your mind, but she sure as hell did something to you. Tell me I'm wrong, lover boy."

" 'Someone special'?" Angus said incredulously. "So you *are* sleeping with my brother."

Jonathan exaggeratedly slapped his palm to his forehead. "I forgot. I'm flaming gay and your brother's spending more time with me than with you. Of *course* we fucked." His hand slid back into his mass of kinky curls—suddenly, he was reminded he desperately needed a haircut and that he'd wasted the money he could have spent on the aforementioned trim on this asshole of a homophobe—and he continued, ditching his hyperbolic sarcasm, "Teenagers these days. Not everyone is fucking each other's brains out. Christ, don't make me lose my opinion of you."

"He stays at your place almost every night."

"He's not exactly comfortable with his family anymore. I'm sure you agree."

Angus's voice quieted. They had finally breached the serious shit. "That doesn't give him the right to ditch us without any explanation."

"I've told him that. He won't hear it." After receiving a disbelieving scowl, Jonathan took a swig of his cooled-down coffee and delved into his character study of Giles Speare. "Giles doesn't like to mince words. He likes to make what he does say count."

"I know that already—"

"He's trying to make a statement with his actions. It might not be the best of moral decisions—which is shockingly out of character for him to you, perhaps—but I suppose you can call it a belated teenage rebellion. Only, you know, he's nineteen and has full responsibility for himself. And before you say anything, I'm not encouraging him to do this or that. I freely admit that I might have exposed him to a lifestyle that might seem distasteful to you and your family. For that, I apologize—although I may insert an argument or two that Giles could have found me repulsive and not have continued along the Yellow Brick Road with me longer than necessary, but I digress. Beyond that exposure, he has made all his decisions without my influence, but with my support. I like your brother, and he's a smart guy, admittedly the smartest guy I know. I'll support whatever choice he makes. Please do the same."

His speech seemed to have gone a little over Angus's head. Nonplussed and a little mortified, Angus replied, "I'm not even sure what he did, exactly."

Jonathan was not surprised. He still hoped his address back there would not be wasted. "Speculate all you want; I'm not telling you. Informing you is another choice Giles must make. I'm pulling a Pontius Pilate and washing my hands of this. Family drama was never my forte. I'm sorry."

"I'm not going to just excuse you." Angus's rage still hadn't fully extinguished, apparently. "Take some responsibility. My mother's worried shitless, and my father doesn't even know what to make of him, all after you took him under your wing."

Jonathan stifled a giggle at the concept. "I haven't taken him under my wing or any of that stuff. I haven't taught him anything. We're friends. From what I know of Giles, he hasn't made many of those before." *Be a little grateful.*

"We were perfectly fine without you," he muttered.

"Your family was an explosion waiting to happen, and Giles knew it." Jonathan didn't want to be too harsh; had he crossed the line?

COMPLEXES

Cautiously quiet, he added, "I'm sorry, that's just the way things are."

Angus watched him with his jaw slightly dropped and his eyebrows knitted together as though the rest of his body rejected whatever his ears just reported. He was very coarse, with a sandpaper personality that only a select few tough-skinned cats liked to rub against. Though mature for his age, his eyes were still young—younger than Giles's, with more earth behind them. Still, Jonathan, with the delicate love of a child who only liked red M&Ms, could pick out the similarities: their slight jaw, their mother's eyelashes, their annoyed eyebrow twitch and slightly crooked teeth. Angus and Giles.

With a loud scraping and a fumble for his coat, Angus stood up and stuck his hands deep inside his pockets. His mouth snapped shut; his lips were as dry as his sympathies. Jonathan didn't even merit a look in the eye as he said, "Take the fucking coffee like you took my brother, you faggot."

The city-goers surrounding them stared, mouths in "O" and eyes in "o." The café's door jingled merrily and slammed furiously, and Angus was gone.

"Ouch," Jonathan said with a sheepish laugh, to diffuse the sudden awkwardness of the situation. A few kindly onlookers gave him empathetic smiles and cheerful words before returning to their lives with a strange anecdote molding in their pockets. Had Giles

CHAPTER ONE

been in his brother's situation, he would have seized both cups of coffee and left, wordlessly. That much, Jonathan knew for certain.

Nevertheless, he was never one to dwell—more like, he preferred *not* to—so he accepted Angus's generously offered coffee and returned via a different route to the Complexes. He was in a particularly peeved mood, so he bestowed one of the cups to a shivering mess of newspapers on the sidewalk. It murmured its faint thanks. Maybe that would dispel the bad karma thickening around him.

Jonathan didn't want to entertain the idea that what he was doing was wrong, immoral, home wrecking, potentially scarring for all party members involved. What he had said to Angus was the unadulterated truth: Giles made all those decisions himself. Granted, in the beginning Jonathan prompted him to let a little loose. He should have remembered from Boy Scouts that once one knot unravels, the rest are quick to follow suit.

But the guy *needed* that loosening up. When Jonathan first noticed him, his intuition whispered that the perfect place for a date with him would be at a nice spa with an hour-long massage or an exotic Chinese acupuncture with atmospheric music playing in the background. Yoga in the sunset. Deep breathing at the very least, if he wasn't that into the rest. He spotted Giles again in one of his Oration classes, and again on the subway home, and again in the same elevator, and again in the same hallway. A couple of accidental encounters were nothing, but as the numbers rose, Jonathan could basically hear the higher beings pleading with him to tap that rock in the right places and make a sculpture. (Jonathan admitted, in the longer hours of his showers, that that particular metaphor made him jittery with the excitement of excellent comparisons and stupid innuendos.)

It was easier than he expected. A little intelligent conversation, some booze, a smoky room, and good music—altogether, in that order, timed perfectly. Then Giles started openly stepping on his own landmines just to marvel at the mushroom clouds, and, well, now Jonathan had a sixteen-year-old hounding him.

He might have helped Giles step out of the sexual closet, but he certainly had *not* slept with him.

Not yet, anyway.

His phone vibrated against his leg, in a Morse code-esque pattern indicating that Giles was on the other end. The deep velvet of his voice, no matter how distorted by the connection, was enough to blast that bratty Angus away into a shadow of an afterthought.

"Pick me up. I think taxi drivers are on strike again. They're all ignoring me."

Jonathan saw a lady stumble over her heels into a very convenient taxi. "How sad you are. You know I don't own a car and— oh—there goes that lady in that taxi just now.

CHAPTER ONE

Either he wasn't in the union, or he didn't get the chain mail."

"I'll pay you back." Fumbling, less ambience, radio. Giles had found himself a taxi after all. "Where are you?"

"I'm outside of Starbucks, right where your brother pissed his teenage ignorance all over me."

Blatantly, Giles disregarded that. "There are legions of them. Starbucks, I mean."

"I know—so meet me at the Complexes."

"I'm not homebound." He could be so damn stubborn. You could offer him a billion dollars and he'd still refuse to return to what he called "an apartment housing narcotic Australians LARP-ing as a family." "I'll stay at your place for the night."

Jonathan teased, "That's basically homebound."

He got a scoff in reply, but no denial. Oh, how Jonathan thrived on the little things.

Sometimes he had to try very, very hard to remind himself that he wasn't taking advantage of Giles's situation to fulfill his fostering attraction. Jonathan would catch him speaking to—or flirting with—another guy, and he'd grapple with his morals. He hadn't *made* Giles bisexual; he'd confessed to finding himself enticed by other passerby males in the past. A little of poking and prodding and rebellion had cracked his nervous shell, is all. There was nothing wrong with that. *You're living in the city, not the boondocks, for godssake. Gays are an essential part of the diverse culture.*

COMPLEXES

Sometimes Jonathan regretted catching his bottomless eyes staring at him through the closing elevator doors.

Punctual as ever, Giles's timed his arrival at the Complexes perfectly to Jonathan's. "Thank you," he said, stepping out of the taxi with the precise regality of a king. "He's paying."

"You owe me big time." Jonathan complied with a wince and waved the driver away before he could realize how measly his tip was.

"I'll never stop owing you, Nathan."

He shouldn't be allowed to say shit like that so casually.

Jonathan hated the nickname but refused to argue for the sake of intimacy. In a rare moment when he happened upon the two Speare brothers together, he noticed that Giles lovingly called Angus "Gus." A gross pet name like that would have pissed off any teenage boy, but even touchy-touchy Angus took it in stride. Giles liked to pull recurring stunts like that, maybe for good-hearted shits and giggles. His execution of said stunts was what remained; he could scrape his nails down a chalkboard with a face that betrayed no knowledge of what a joke is or any awareness that he damaged the ears of anyone at all. In the end, he made music.

Jonathan endured the silence of the brief elevator ride. Giles was utterly absorbed in rummaging through his messenger bag before extracting obviously pirated silver

CHAPTER ONE

DVDs in a black case, which he then held in Jonathan's direction. "The reason I didn't pay for the taxi," he announced matter-of-factly. Jonathan could almost imagine him proposing, diamond ring and all, and saying the exact same thing.

"What movies?"

"I don't know. It's like a grab bag." Only Giles would purchase such a questionable thing as if he were buying a pack of gum.

"More importantly, how much did it cost?"

The elevator whined an off-key *ding!* and they stepped out, Jonathan brandishing the keys to E07. Giles walked and talked, eyes fixed forward as if they were glued in that way. Jonathan wouldn't doubt it if they were. "Enough to be unable to pay for the taxi. Before you criticize my financial decision—"

"—You're entitled to buy what you want; I'm not your overbearing wife—"

"—I just wanted to get it for you."

His pale, freckled face burning, Jonathan fumbled with his keys, dropped them, cursed, and tried opening his stubborn door again. He could feel Giles's eyes fixated on him, probably playing God and prejudging his soul with a wooden mallet of intense justice like they always do, so casually. "And then you make me pay for the taxi," he replied, not maliciously but with force equivalent to the scrutiny he was under.

"Logically, the DVDs will make up for it."

COMPLEXES

"I needed the money for a *haircut*."

"There's perhaps one hundred and fifty in there. I haven't counted yet."

"Who buys one hundred and fifty movies all at once?"

"I did, forty-five minutes ago."

To Jonathan, this was a game of petty frivolities. For all he knew, Giles took it dead seriously. The door shivered open—everything seemed to shiver—and voilà, E07 opened up in all its messy gloriousness. Blank canvases, discarded canvases, books, DVDs, television cables, laptops and their respective chargers—Jonathan owned everything but practicality, save a banged-up microwave and a heater that smoked rather than heated. He originally roomed with an ex-boyfriend, but after their breakup the most useful appliances were neatly packed up and imbued with deadly anti-Jonathan curses.

Many times Giles had had the nerve to tidy up, but Jonathan always met his competition with equal verve. Most everything between the two was a delicate balance: Giles's dark hair, Jonathan's ginger-orange; Giles's order, Jonathan's chaos; Giles's apparent indifference, Jonathan's apparent infatuation; Giles's brevity, Jonathan's verbosity. But when it came to the quality and manner of their words, the balance tipped heavily toward the snark and droll.

"Fuck, it's freezing in here. When was the last time we had heat in here?"

"Never."

CHAPTER ONE

"That was a—"

"—rhetorical question. I'm fully aware."

He could come off as a real asshole sometimes.

Jonathan opened the black packet of ripped-and-burned films and leafed through the identical-looking discs, amused by the sheer number of them. "What are we going to do with all these?"

Giles frowned, disappointed by his friend's lack of common sense. "Watch them."

"All of them?" Sure, Jonathan loved motion pictures, but the very concept of viewing more than a hundred of them was far too tiring. He could certainly comprehend the appeal of the "unknown movie," to a fault.

Despite the cold, that aforementioned fault melted when Giles smiled, charming and crooked.

"It'll make up for that taxi fee. I promise."

Last night Jessie had hit her forehead against her bedroom wall a good twenty times to awaken her brain from its sleepy stupor. The impacts were light enough to not leave a bruise but hard enough to germinate a headache. She curled up in bed, choosing halfheartedly to wait until after therapy to make any life-altering decisions.

Despite Jessie's fantasies of her seventeenth year being a wondrous and happy one, she had lost a lot of friends this year. She couldn't fully explain to herself the behaviors that had pushed them away. She speculated that it was passive-aggressive testing, pushing away. According to Hilde, it was self-care. Either way she felt guilty. Either way she was friendless.

The next day, Jessie emerged from therapy with Hilde, eyes slightly puffy from watering. It was the weekend, and with nothing else to reap from the day, she retired to bed, even though it was bright enough that she could still see her posters of *The Great Wave off Kanagawa* and Green Day.

Angus had texted her, and she responded with a quarter of her already halved will. That a boy was interested in her was a surprise—though it honestly surprised her more that she was rather uninterested. The attention was, admittedly, nice. She hadn't received "good morning" and "sweet dreams" texts since the unspeakable ex-boyfriend. So far she was impressed with her usually fluttering heart's stability in this Angus matter.

Before mild hypertrophic scarring could give it away, Jessie was fast to admit that she suffered from depression and anxiety. Despite that, Angus had no idea. With the unspeakable ex-boyfriend, the depression was as prevalent as blue on a cloudless, sunny day. She only thought it fitting she would keep her mouth shut about it while the sky remained steely gray.

CHAPTER ONE

Diagnosed a mere year ago, Jessie recalled her little depression firsts: taking antidepressants, then taking antipsychotics as supplements to the antidepressants, individual therapy, group therapy, family sessions, dialectical behavioral therapy, art therapy. And all those had to do with recovery.

After burying her face in her pillow to defend from the colorful floaters harassing her eyes, she slept for either a second or an eternity; she woke up after her mother's third try, and trudged out of bed with a throat craving warm beverages. Monday. At least she didn't have after-school obligations on Mondays. Mondays were good.

She would say "Same shit, different day," but that would mean actually professing how boring her daily life was. Assassins and magic and time travelling and the like didn't exist unless you did enough acid, and Jessie valued her sanity (and recovery?) too dearly to embark on such an adventure. Instead, she settled for her morning mocha and her knees tucked into her oversized T-shirt. It was damn cold for early June. Her ankles were numb. Her socks had fallen off in her sleep.

COMPLEXES

Chapter Two

Angus wished he could smoke. He lived the straightedge life of an isolated teenager, lacking the connections or guts to shatter the hazy, drug-addicted sphere. He wanted the fumes to infest his lungs, plague him with a hacking cough, and transform him into a mysterious, short-breathed city-dweller who blew in the faces of those who looked at him the wrong way. It was one of his fears that Giles had gotten the opportunity to try before him—if so, the wish would be promptly abandoned, replaced with something novel that his elder brother would never copy. Seldom did he admit to himself that his wishes and their respective conditions were absurd. But he checked himself, justified himself: this was the way of younger siblings.

After his little argument with the flaming Jonathan, Angus felt the incredible pull of stupidity guiding his impulses. He dared bother Jessie more than often, and he did not feel ashamed to look his mother in the eye when he failed that biology test. These were the subtle signs of brewing storms; one could only weather through the weather. Learning evolution could wait when the sky darkened around the crown of his head.

This dimming of clouds seemed to mirror itself in the weather lately. Angus, though usually extra resistant to the cold, wore multiple layers of clothing, including an olive green scarf his mother knitted that he dug up in a closet at home. It smelled and looked thrifted, and was perhaps the reason why his mother never picked up her needles again. His mom's erratic hobbies, Angus guessed, were the result of boredom as a housewife with two already grown boys. She seemed to live off a bucket list, tasting but not consuming.

Subway doors rattled open and Angus emerged first—like a man on a mission, as he liked to pretend. He climbed the stairs in strides, walked a couple blocks to the Complexes, counting the smokers who killed themselves gradually with fire and freeze outside store entrances. His fingers had just encircled the handle of the door to the apartments when his undertaking was interrupted, almost happily, by a blend of a question and a statement:

"Hey, you. Yeah, stay awhile?"

Angus cranked his head sideways. Disappearing tan, golden hair, eyes the color of the sky during a long lost summer. This boy looked familiar, but Angus's troubled mind could hardly identify anyone that was not Jessie, a relative, or a wannabe relative. "It's cold," Angus responded matter-of-factly, hand clenching the handle a tad more decisively.

"So what?" He breathed smelly fumes diagonally. He proffered a box of Marlboros with a Santa-like generosity. Angus's grip on the door loosened. His fingers, presently occupied by a paper cylinder, shook toward his mouth. The boy with the inherited winning grin lighted him up. Angus breathed, grimaced, and coughed, seemingly all at once. The boy laughed good-naturedly.

"I'm Antony."

"Angus."

"I don't usually smoke, but it's one of those days, you know?"

"I know." He didn't.

They proceeded to relate to each other on multiple levels, some of which were imagined, for both boys wished to impress the other. Angus felt drawn to Antony's charisma; in turn, Angus's background intrigued Antony. Together, they would eventually count the clouds around each other's temples and seek their destinies in their shapes. But for now, they only wished for a certain degree of companionship, the same kind every smoker lent to another when a cigarette is passed. After the obligatory conversation about school and the weather died, Antony invited Angus to his apartment.

"My dad's out, so we can hang unbothered," he explained as they warmed their bodies by taking the stairs. Angus would never have guessed that Antony was nervous; the latter spun his key ring on his pinky finger out of anxiety, not out of confidence. Something about Angus seemed fragile—not like porcelain, but like a shrapnel bomb.

"It's really not much, but it is home for now." Antony gave the sticking door a good shove before entering E11. It was considerably smaller and less homey than its counterparts, partly due to its splitting space with the washing room. The Shepherds owned more containers than they did things that needed containing; Angus thus quickly concluded that they either lived a vagabond sort of life, were very poor indeed, or both. Perhaps Antony's raggedy jeans weren't a simple fashion statement.

Angus asked, mostly for the sake of discourse, "When did you move here again?"

"Two weeks ago. Want a breakfast burrito?"

He refused, and continued in a most earnest tone, "I'm sorry, I'm trying to remember why I didn't notice your family move in."

"It's just me and my dad, I wouldn't call us a 'family,' per se," Antony said, distractedly stabbing at the microwave. "Your mom noticed. She gave us cookies. Nice lady." He then craned his neck and squinted at Angus. "I might be missing something, but you don't look half Indian, though. You're as white as white can get."

Angus strained his memory to recall, what, exactly, was happening two Wednesdays ago. School, the cold trek home, the cold home, and cold fingers doing homework with his ear against the wall, waiting for Giles to return home. His mother did say something, something about Ruthy, the sour woman living in E06. "I guess my mom did greet you." He absentmindedly resigned himself to this fuzzy sequence of events. More attentively, he responded to Antony: "My dad's Australian.

36

COMPLEXES

Don't get me started on how the two could possibly meet."

"How did the two meet?" The emerging microwavable meal smelled of pure heat.

Angus grimaced and struggled to find the most sociable picket of his fence. "It's personal."

"Nah, man," Antony nonchalantly attempted to disperse his worries. "It's your parents' business, not yours."

"I make it my business."

Antony had pricked himself on one of Angus's barbs, but he was born of steel skin. Without asking for permission, like an author running on stolen inspiration, he conveyed his assumptions of his lacking parentage. His challenge, relayed via his piercing eyes, was intended not to undermine Angus's argument, but to corroborate it. "It's not that I don't make it my business anymore," Antony explained. "The point is, my dad and I, we're two different people who just happen to have similar DNA. Sure, all the shit that he does affects me, but only because I let it affect me, you know?"

"I don't know." Angus scowled, hearing the uncertainty in his own voice. "If you really must insist, my father was on some sort of a humanitarian trip to India when they met. They fell in love there, and I guess, they got married. Though they were both pretty young at the time." Only now did the story seem bizarre to him; it was almost as if his father were doing his mother a favor by shipping her away from the third-world slums. As if their marriage were simply an act of generosity, not an act of love. Logically, Angus acknowledged that these thoughts were speculation, simply carbonated bubbles atop a soda; emotionally, it was wishful thinking on his part. A divorce would be the generous thing for them to do right now.

"Why do you want to know?" Angus inquired.

Antony responded dismissively, "The walls here are thin, and rumors are like pervading air."

"What bullshit did people dream up this time?" Neighbors in the city were no different than neighbors living acres away back in Australia: they both were nosy. Plus, Angus knew they couldn't simply up and away in a grayscale hot air balloon to Oz like last time.

"Do you want me to be real for a second here?" Antony inclined his head, wondering if the wire he had chosen would detonate the bomb.

Angus said, in a questionable tone, "I thought we were being real already."

"Right, right. But I mean, real, for real." He swallowed, fumbling with the words in his mouth only to catch them with the tip of his tongue. "I hear it's fragile over in E01. That … let's say, if a home wrecker would get involved, he'd only have to breathe a little deeply to get the job done. I'm a little nervous talking to you, actually. You seem on edge, and I'm guessing family stuff is pushing you cliff-ways." Exhaling, he braced himself for an impending verbal explosion.

COMPLEXES

The bomb sighed but moved no further. Antony had somehow defused him. "You're right; someone's wrecking something. I really don't know if I should tell you this stuff. We're still trying to sort it out ourselves."

"I understand, I understand." Antony retreated, chewing on the firsthand scraps of information. Someone was wreaking havoc on the Speare family, and it wasn't Gerard. Not wishing to push his luck, Antony decided to abandon the campaign and pursue an optional objective instead: becoming friends with Angus. The eternal winter wasn't going to recede; the keen social instinct within him knew that. If he was going to be trapped within the Complexes, allies would be better than enemies.

The drinks came out rather fast. It began with Antony's offer—for there was nothing but water, milk, and beer to drink—and with Angus's curiosity, bred of his only having tasted the wine at Sunday liturgy. The beer, to him, tasted uncomfortable, but he drank it anyway, hoping that the following sip would be comfortable. Angus marveled at alcoholics and their resilience whilst consuming the disgusting stuff, without knowing that such resilience was learned and he was learning it now.

Antony also disliked drinking—his father only did so while watching sports games late at night—but he wanted to loosen up his to-be companion. When the weather was warmer, he would go to those teenage parties, drink enough to skim the surface of drunk, and watch the girls. Wasted girls were unleashed, loudmouthed, and soft-lipped. It partly worried him that he enjoyed exercising dominance over confused, twittering birds. Not that he ever did—it was just a strange fantasy of his.

None of the above, however, was discussed while drinking. Small talk was made once again, about the warmer life. "My dad owned a resort in the Malaysian islands," Angus explained, "No good once it got cold. Some summers he would let me and my brother run amok there. We'd pester all the carnies and tourists and pretend we were sleeping on the rides when the camera took pictures. We would have gotten kicked out and banished if it weren't for our owning the place; we'd climb the roller coasters and walk them, that's why. It was sort of like a dare. My brother was never afraid, though. Those days—those days were fun."

"My dad and I—yeah, you probably guessed—we're vagrants. We used to stay in one place for longer, maybe two years. We stayed in Seattle, Frisco, and then all the way to Chicago, you name it. I always helped out by working. Babysitting, mostly, when I was younger. I would be a no-good tutor, so it was the only option for me. Once, I babysat this adorable little girl. Only problem was that she was seven and wasn't potty-trained yet. When I changed her diapers I felt like a real child-pedo, you know what I mean? I wonder how she is now—if she's still adorable and if her parents still hire creepy dudes off craigslist to change her diapers."

COMPLEXES

Angus would have laughed tentatively, but the giggles emerged like vomit from his mouth. Antony appreciated this exchange and showed his gratitude by raising his bottle and taking a deep swig of beer. "This stuff is disgusting," he commented.

"I was going to say that," Angus said enthusiastically, surprised that his companion blurted it out first. "I guess I'm just not a beer kind of guy."

Antony tilted his head respectfully toward him. "First time drinking?"

"Yeah … smoking, too." Immediately, red flushed up to Angus's pale face. He hadn't meant to say that, Antony noticed, but he couldn't think of anything to ease Angus's sudden nervousness. His silence would have to suffice—but it didn't. Angus was utterly embarrassed to be caught, cherry popped, with a stranger who would then introduce him to a world of substances he had previously shut himself out from. But there was something more …there was always something more.

"Thanks, but no thanks," Angus said, standing up, empty-handed. "Your—fucking—*indoctrination* isn't going to work on me." He fumbled with the doorknob, then made a point to slam the door shut. The resonating noise rang with what was supposed to sound like finality. Antony heard heavy footsteps down the hallway and another door.

He sniffed, shrugged, put the bottle down. Something was going on in E01, and something Antony did or said had influenced

CHAPTER TWO

Angus somehow. That's all he figured. Antony wasn't one to overthink—at least, not when problems became drinking buddies.

    Mara had just finished crying when the door opened. The back of her hand clumsily swatted away her sadness as Giles entered, for the first time in a week. Wednesday ... he'd probably run out of clothes to wear and needed to pick up a bundle more while leaving his laundry behind for Mara handle on Sunday. Like a scavenger following the trail of breadcrumbs, Mara would systematically check every pocket for evidence of where Giles had been. Tissues frequented, concert tickets were rarer, but most jarring to her were the occasionally forgotten condoms. She couldn't fathom why her son would need them—for sex, obviously—but her fluttering chest denied that three-letter word's existence in the same way James denied her in bed.

    Attempting to appear less puffy-eyed and snot-nosed, Mara straightened the wrinkles from her shirt and addressed her son with careful words: "I've missed you."

    Giles paused. "Good afternoon," he said. He, usually silent, wasn't often caught in want of words.

    "Is that all you have to say? You leave me hanging for a week and all you say is that? I know you're next door with that Jonathan boy; I know the trouble you boys can get up to. Don't pretend like I'm the Virgin Mary, as if you get to

42

leave little surprises in your pockets like you left shit in the diaper as an infant. Don't act civil, we're beyond that. Some yelling in this house would do us some good."

But she didn't say that, of course. Her tongue was leashed to her teeth. "Just check your jeans pockets for money when you leave them in the hamper," she said numbly, pretending that his habits were endearing. "You always leave a couple of dollars here and there."

Giles's feet padded toward his room, which was largely untouched. "I will," he answered not before deliberately hesitating to examine her choice of words. Certainly Mara would find his pockets empty this Sunday. Giles's door opened and closed, softly, and she leaned forward, her back a lopsided arch, into her hands, rough with dishwashing and mothering and weathering.

To distract herself, she baked more cookies. It was mindless work. The chocolate chip delicacies disappeared slowly during the week; even if no one stated it, the two remaining men in the house appreciated her for her seemingly happy resilience. At least, that's how she optimistically interpreted the empty cookie jar.

Giles exited his room, a large red bag, undoubtedly filled with another week's worth of clothes, weighing down his right shoulder. He would have left wordlessly had Angus not stormed in, basically breathing thunderclouds.

CHAPTER TWO

"What are you doing here?" Angus snapped.

"Retrieving some clothes."

"Mom hates doing your laundry." He jabbed at any weak point he could find, like a mosquito hungering for a clothed man's skin.

Sensing that this altercation might last awhile, Giles shrugged his bag off his shoulder. "Do you hate doing my laundry?"

It took Mara a moment to realize that Giles had addressed her. She debated her answer, fingers wrapped around cookie dough. "I don't particularly enjoy doing laundry," Mara carefully said, hoping that her confidence would match her son's deep voice.

Giles raised his eyebrows at his younger sibling. "That means yours, too, Angus."

"Don't try to joke around with me. You're practically living with him; do your laundry with his." Jonathan's name was decidedly taboo in E01.

He contemplated this. Mara guessed at his thoughts. *To alienate yourself further or to keep hanging on a thread?* The thought processing of both her sons came easily to her. It was the actual answer that came hard as a brass-knuckled punch.

With a sideways look to his mother, Giles said ambiguously, "I'm sure she wouldn't mind for a couple of weeks."

Mara concentrated on extracting the dough squares from the package onto the glossy sheet. Angus threw her a pleading look before throwing his hands up, surrendering.

44

COMPLEXES

Satisfied with the silent outcome, Giles retrieved his bag, readjusted the strap, and then curiously paused close in front of his brother. Taking a whiff, he announced loudly, "A little strange of you to be drinking, Gus."

With that, Giles was gone.

Angus looked piteously at his mother as he searched for an explanation. "That new kid—that kid next door, he—"

"You don't have to explain yourself," Mara interrupted strongly. "You boys are old enough to make your own decisions. It's just a beer with our new neighbor."

"No, that's not fair to you. I don't want to become like another Giles."

Mara gazed blankly at her hands, soiled slightly with sweet dough. "You're not like him, Angus. I've told you that ever since you were little, you know that." She recalled the late nights spent in Angus's bedroom, consoling him for getting an A instead of an A+ in fifth grade mathematics. Giles got the A+, he'd say. Not worthy, he'd say. Not good enough. Reminiscing, things were easier when Angus wanted to be just like his older brother.

At her words, Angus tossed her a pained yet understanding expression; she caught it and blinked back tears, pretending as though her eyelashes could embrace her son. "If you can," she said, concealing a sniff, "can you run to the store and buy some more milk? We're running out, and I expect you'd want some with the cookies."

CHAPTER TWO

Angus was all too eager to occupy himself with errands. Mara started to cry again when he exited, just as she did whenever the heavy loneliness descended upon her like a cartoon anvil, covering her life in a steady gradient of gray. Once the cookies began baking in the oven, Mara found herself at the door of Giles's room, hand reaching like God in *The Creation of Adam* toward the knob.

The door surrendered to her pull, and all the world behind her seemed to collapse as the room revealed itself to her. When was the last time she'd been in here? Remembering anything but to breathe was difficult—she needed something, some hint of her son's old life.

She overturned the trash bin, slid open drawers, fingered through pages of numerous books, and checked the pockets of jackets, all with increasing intensity. Mara sniffed the bed and realized with a sense of uninterpretable doom that it stank strongly of Giles's cologne, as if he had intended it to smell that way. She checked the cavern underneath his bed, opened dusty shoe boxes, and picked up and put down picture frames occupied by tired posed photos of her son receiving his First Communion. Though she discovered small but empty double picture frame that opened like a diptych with a latch, she couldn't remember for the life of her what belonged there.

It was when she opened a DVD case of a long forgotten rock band's live performance. A card stumbled out and fluttered drunkenly in midair before falling flat on its face. Only by reading it could she recall sifting through shelves of neatly organized condolences for the perfect piece of folded stock paper on which to convey her good wishes. For Giles's high school graduation, she had written:

I love you and I am proud of you, for all the big things and all the tiny things you probably have forgotten about by now. I will never forget how tall and awkward you looked in your uniform on your first day, and now how you've filled in every inch of your shoes and how your shoulders match the seams of your shirts. Now, you're able to move on to great and wonderful Oz-worthy things! Revel in today; you can only take certain steps in life once.

The other two messages, from Angus and James, were brief and hardly noteworthy as compared to Mara's. She was an overly proud mother, who literally swelled when Giles gave his speech as valedictorian. "That's my son," she wanted to say. "That's my son who used to squeeze my hand too tightly when he went trick-or-treating. He burst from my womb with a rage, and now he's seizing the world as his birthright."

Mara wanted to still be proud of him. He was still bright and wise, after all. But how could she be proud of a boy she no longer knew? How could she wash the clothes of a man who had carelessly shed them on the floor of countless motel rooms? It wasn't that she had high standards for the boy—it was that he was gone in almost every sense of the word, too thin and too ashamed to yank his chin up and tell his mother how much he'd changed.

The passive-aggressive fighting wore her out, and yet she contributed to it by rummaging through Giles's room. She placed the card back in its dark, enclosed case, and used her hip to slide shut the drawer. A dam was built behind her eyes; she couldn't bring herself to tear. After stealing a final sweeping look at the room, she was called by the returning Angus to the kitchen. The cookies were burning.

❄❄❄❄❄

Morrissey insisted upon everyone's attending her sixth-grade poetry night. She did beg the attendance from every person on the floor by discreetly slipping flyers in the cracks of the doors. On her important night, Wednesday night, she sported a carefully selected tan tank top, black leggings, laced-up Converse, and a slouchy hat. Indeed, she looked very artsy and poetic for a twelve-year-old.

"Look at you, Morrissey!" Gerard exclaimed his excitement for the night just as loudly as a band of bagpipes. Much to her discontent, he plucked her up and spun her about like the little girl he imagined her to be. "You could be a real art student dressed like that."

Back on the floor, Morrissey huffed her blonde bangs from her face. "Why do we have to stereotype art students? I bet they dress all sorts of ways." More eagerly, she bent herself sideways to check the outcome of all her soliciting. Bending down to her short stature, Antony waved to her from behind his father. "Where's everyone?" she asked, considering the hallway empty.

"Excuse *me*," Antony mumbled, sourly ignored.

"Morrissey, I don't think anyone else will be coming. Other people have lives too, remember?" Ruthy explained from the kitchen. Antony bypassed Morrissey and Gerard and reached for the fruits and crackers his aunt was preparing. She slapped his hand away without even a second glance. "Don't be rude, these are for the guests and the other sixth-graders."

Morrissey approached the neat setup of biscuits, strawberries, grapes, pepperoni, and cheese. "My teacher asked us to make 'whores devours' to make it super classy."

"*Hors d'oeuvres*, dear," Ruthy corrected her, devouring a laugh. After readjusting the biscuits, she wrapped the dish and gingerly placed it in a tote bag. "We'll be off now. Her school is just a subway ride away."

Gerard, the last to leave the apartment, closed the door behind him. "So what's happening tonight, anyway? You didn't specify in the invitation—"

"Yeah, I'd like to know what I'm getting myself into," Antony grumbled. For the occasion, he was forced to wear his nice khakis and button-up shirt. Not that he didn't like to dress up; it was that he knew no continuum of proper dress. He either dressed entirely casually or entirely formally; this combination he now exhibited was a strange mix he typically associated with four-eyed hipsters who carried their noses in the air.

Bopping his son on the head, Gerard continued, "Is it original poetry or just a recitation?"

"Wow, you sound like you know your stuff," Morrissey commented. Gerard shrugged, recalling months of attending poetry readings reminiscent of the Beat Generation in Frisco with her. A lot of *Howls* were reproduced, but she obsessed over the slams that she loved. She even insisted on Gerard giving poetry a shot, but he never did.

"You listening? Yeah, it's all original, written by us in class and stuff. I've been working on my repertoire all year, but since there are so many kids, I can't recite all that I want to recite. It sucks because they suck at poetry."

"Let the other kids have a go at it; they're all not born poets like you," Ruthy suggested, amused at her daughter's superiority complex. In response, Morrissey simply rolled her eyes and nodded a *Yes, Mother*.

The walk to the subway was brief, and the subway ride was slightly less. The entire time, Gerard was engulfed in thoughts of the past, leaking like pearly raindrops.

The midday harbored a beautiful city, and within the city, Gerard and Alice, who wrapped each other in linen and legs. "Let's do something," Alice suggested, with a stretch of her tattooed limbs. "I've been meaning to visit this poetry café."

COMPLEXES

And so they dressed for a night outing, Alice in that beige-white that always looked stunning against her fair skin, in a dress that weaved together thinly and draped downward like a dream catcher. With her hand in his, they traipsed across the city, bumping into enough friends to create a following to the café. They arrived a tad late and thus had to stand in the back to listen to the poets.

"For that pretty lady in the back, with the little rack that I appreciate and he appreciates, too:

Undertaker embrace you! That's right, go fuck yourself in the dirt! I'd appreciate that and I'm sure the crowd would, too.

Chimera beauty; I made love to a woman with Medusa's head, and into stone I become, head enlarged beyond Rushmore and genitals sawed off.

Keep your cat to yourself; for I found out I have AIDs!"

The crowd laughed sympathetically and gave the man the hearty applause he deserved. Every so often Gerard would snake his hand around Alice's neck and kiss her temple, his place of worship. There they remained all night, past aching feet and taut smiles. "I'm really glad we came," she commented with a whisper in between poems, while an ambient band played strange jingles.

CHAPTER TWO

They returned home slowly, Gerard grasping the back of her dress as pleadingly as a mute dog. Sometimes she'd give in and they would make love in an alley, breathing smothered breaths but exuding aroused passion. Most nights she'd tease him until they got home, ripple the bedsheets with her hands until Gerard could not contain himself any longer. He'd kiss her, massage her breasts underneath her dress, and recite Cummings' poems to her ear.

"Dad."

Antony shattered the reverie.

"This is our stop," he said, tilting his head toward the open subway door. Gerard hurried out behind him, hands sweaty in his pockets though the cold nipped at his cheeks. The troupe walked two blocks before finally entering the school gymnasium, warm with yellow tones that all school gyms seemed to possess. Ruthy uncovered her dish and set it at one of the tables as Morrissey rushed to join her fellow classmates at the bleachers. With nowhere else to go, Gerard and Antony covered paper plates in food and sat in a pair of metal chairs. Around them, the audience slowly grew to fill up the make-shift amphitheater.

"How was school? You fitting in all right? Any weird kids with stories to tell?" Gerard asked after digging into the modest amount of "whores devours" on his plate.

Antony's plate, on the other hand, was quite stacked. "School's school. I'm not super tight with anyone, but I'm not worried about that shit, you know me. Only story I've got is about Angus."

COMPLEXES

"Angus the beef or Angus Speare?"

"Angus the beef with a spear up his ass." Antony ran his tongue across his teeth before taking a bite in a mini cracker-pepperoni-cheese sandwich he had created. Swallowing, he continued, "He even took the spear out of his ass and started attacking me with it."

"Really? What did he do?"

"Yeah, uh, I invited him up to our apartment, and things were cool, you know? We talked for a bit, and then I gave him a beer—his first time having a beer and all—and we talked some more. Then he suddenly flips a shit. I remember exactly what he said, this huge word: *indoctrination*. I mean, what does that even mean?"

Gerard responded with a smile, "It's kind of like brainwashing, if he used it in a negative sense."

"So I was brainwashing him by giving him a drink? I think I'm missing something here."

Father and son were about to begin piecing their puzzle together to find missing links when the event began. An older woman, erudite and tall in stature, asked everyone to take their seats and delivered a concise introduction to the program. Each of the thirty sixth-graders would speak at least once, all with their own, original work, ranging from free verse to sonnets. Finally, she bowed out and allowed her students to take the stage.

Gerard smiled as the first young boy adjusted the microphone stand to his height. He was strangely excited—he hadn't given a second glance to poetry since his time with Alice. No doubt, the words and structure would be on the level of a middle schooler, but he cherished it all the same, just as a thinker appreciates the shortcomings of the scientific approach.

Most memorable, of course, were Morrissey's poems. She assertively advanced toward the crowd and read from her paper without consulting it often. Her poem, *Basil, Sage, and Oregano,* began thus:

"On a microwave with an incomplete countdown

A fraternal triplet stands like sleeping sentinels

Accented with Mexican-like shades:

Beige and red, beige and green, beige and tan

And dotted grotesquely by sticky,

Brown sauce covered fingerprints

They are tiny treasure chests playing the role of a heartthrob

The mysterious Mr. Tall-Dark-and-Handsome

Sheltering three groundbreaking secrets in his breast

Enticing the heroine.

Basil, Sage, and Oregano
Steal me away to Scarborough Fair
(Or was it a different three?)
Perhaps they are blessed herbs
A hint at my mother's witchcraft
Or the reason behind my cousin's

54

COMPLEXES

Meticulously locked doors?
Maybe poison and drugs
Purposefully mislabeled but forgotten
Like a snake with undiscovered venom
Conserved in his glands
They could be traditional spices
Smuggled from Saudi Arabia
A successful robber's pride
Contained in a mundane kitchen
Like rusted trophies concealed
Behind books on dusty shelves.

Perhaps they are not even herbs!
Ashes of a traitor combusted at the stake,
Gathered by a great-grandmother, who watched
As Mary watched her Son on the cross.
Or rather, little men caged in impenetrable ceramic
Each possessing a purpose:
Basil, a crowned king
Sage, a wise monk
Oregano, a farmer from Oregon.

Or maybe they are empty
Just three jars—bodies with no souls
Waiting to be soaked in material, in life
In meaning, in maturing, in accomplishment,
In aging, in dwindling, in barrenness
Once again.

All it takes is a twist of the wrist
A little force to unveil the contents

CHAPTER TWO

To sniff whatever aroma, to perceive whatever colors,

To taste whatever bitterness, to feel whatever coarseness

But, like an ashamed child, I avert my eyes

For conspiracy is more enjoyable than the truth."

Morrissey descended from the stage, her beam as bright as smelting metal. Antony fidgeted through the rest of the show, occasionally commenting on the idiosyncrasies of each child. That girl's mother still decides her outfits. His voice will crack into a newscaster's. She's meant to be dancing on the stage, not chewing and spitting out her awkward teenage sonnets. Eventually Gerard lightly bumped the back of his head to signify that he had had enough of his bizarre judgments.

"How did I do?" Morrissey inquired after the show, stepping on the backs of Antony's knockoff Converse sneakers. "Were my poems good? Aren't they great? Did you recognize who they were inspired by? That 'Oregano farmer from Oregon' joke sure was funny, wasn't it?"

"It was." Gerard laughed spirit into his lie. More truthfully, he added, "Like your mother said: you were born to write poetry."

Morrissey ceased antagonizing her cousin as she chewed on that compliment. "But what if I don't want to be poet?"

He considered this. "Then you were born to do whatever you want to do."

COMPLEXES

She scoffed wisely. "You're a people pleaser, Uncle. A lying, rotten, people pleaser. Okay, I was born to write poetry, but I think I'll write prose just to spite you." With that, she walked faster than her company, the lamb leading the sheep just to show that she knew how. Ruthy exchanged cautious looks with Gerard; now they both knew that she was as sharp as a scalpel.

But Antony continued to handle her as if he was asking to be pricked. "If you're so smart," he said accusingly, "Why do you ask me weird questions? With your knowledge and with Internet access, you could have all the answers you'd ever need."

Morrissey pivoted and looked up at him, eyes narrowed and teasing. "It's because I'm so smart that I like to ask you questions. You'll understand when you're older. Speaking of questions, mind if I ask another one? Why are sixth-grade boys so stupid?"

"Easy," Antony replied. "It's because boys mature loads slower than girls do."

"Do you think sixth-grade boys know they mature, as you say, loads slower than girls do?"

"Yeah, I did when I was in sixth grade."

"So is it a fact or an excuse?"

"Uh—"

They arrived at the Complexes and crammed into what had to be the slowest elevator in the city. Accompanying them was an elderly man clinging to his walker and the one and only Mara Speare, ladling in her arms a tote filled with late-night groceries. Gerard noticed bags, heavy underneath her glazed-over eyes, and her lips, chapped from the cold. "Let me help you with those," he proposed, thus interrupting his, Morrissey's, and Antony's intellectual bickering.

The fog clouding her dark eyes cleared at the sound of his offering help. "Oh. Yes. Thank you," she murmured, allowing some of the weight cradled in her arms to tumble into Gerard. The elevator beeped, passing floor B.

"—Like I said before, it's not an excuse; it's a well-known scientific fact," insisted Antony, somewhere far away from Gerard's current state of mind. His arm brushed Mara's as he lightly tugged the sack away from her. From the bottoms of his eyes, he could see some of the bag's contents: milk, rice, strawberries, some unknown meat. She returned to her blank state as she made use of what little space she possessed and flapped her undoubtedly sore arms.

"What's for dinner tonight?" Gerard asked, as casually as a husband.

Mara blinked, then smiled courteously, lips stretching over her teeth. "Tomorrow's dinner. Miso salmon." They passed floor C.

Morrissey countered, her voice now excitable, "It's a fact that boys use to their advantage to act dumber than they really are. The very fact that they're using science as an excuse for their antics is indicative of their disguised smartness."

"Whoa, I don't even know what the fuck you said."

COMPLEXES

Ruthy interjected by violently pulling Antony's ear. "Watch your mouth around my daughter, or I'll start calling you things you've never even dreamed of."

Blatantly disregarding them, Gerard fumbled for an extended exchange with the object of his strange affections. "Sounds delicious. Are you one of those cooks who learn from a recipe or do you just wing it?"

Mara indicated a piece of paper tucked in between her groceries. "I learn from the best," she said, admitting to her online recipe hunting. "I wasn't born to be a cook, but somehow much of my time these days is dedicated to it." The elevator squeaked past floor D. The elderly man with the walker exited at a much faster speed than his body seemed to allow.

"Well"—Gerard slowly contemplated her statement, which revealed to him a crack in the atmosphere of her world—"just because you were born to do something, doesn't mean you'll do it. I suppose the same thing applies backwards, right?"

Behind closed lips, Mara laughed lightly. "I suppose you're right."

Meanwhile, Antony nursed his ear. "Aunt Ruthy, isn't that a tad hypocritical of you? Just a tad?"

"I really don't care," said Ruthy bluntly.

"Ha! I win!" exclaimed Morrissey.

"What a rowdy elevator we have here," Mara remarked just as the doors opened to floor E. "Thank you for helping." Not so eager to

CHAPTER TWO

part ways, Gerard offered to carry her groceries to her apartment. She didn't seem to mind.

The elevator emptied its contents onto the hallway, where they dispersed. With every step came growing anticipation: what would the apartment look like? Did she decorate it with goods from trips to India? Will she invite me to stay awhile, maybe share a glass of wine? Am I overstepping my boundaries here?

Mara unlocked the door and allowed Gerard to enter first. "Here's home," she said, eyes on him. "You can put the bag on the table. I'll take care of it."

When he passed Mara and stepped across the threshold of their apartment, his eyes were slapped onto the image of James Speare, sitting at a table with his untouched dinner. He was only slightly bulky, in the way that his shoulders were broad and his stomach filled his shirt. His harsh and narrow brown eyes were made harsher by his strong jaw and stiff bottom lip. His hands were large, and, Gerard guessed, would be very intimidating if they were balled into fists. He noticed that James was scrutinizing him as well; he wondered what kind of persona was imagined for him.

Literally watching his step, he placed the overflowing bag onto the table, across from James. "Hello, Mr. Speare, right?"

"James," he responded, his voice at least a notch or two deeper than Gerard's. Standing up, he shook Gerard's hand and gave it a good squeeze before releasing him. "I see you've met my wife, Mara."

COMPLEXES

"Yes—she welcomed us when we moved in a while back." Gerard desperately wanted to look at Mara, the astonishingly pretty wife, but he feared that breaking eye contact with James would signal disrespect. Something about that man's aura informed him that the very concept of respect was observed very carefully in E01. "You've got a better view of the city over here than I do," he said, gesturing to the window. Gerard had hoped his last statement had a humbling effect.

"Mm. It is a decent view."

"Gerard," Mara said, entering her apartment like a mother bird to her nest (meanwhile, he tingled not with humility when she said his name), "thank you again for helping. Sometimes I pick out far too much at the store."

Pleased with his effect on Mara but frightened of James's disquieting gaze, he decided not to overstay his welcome. "It's really no problem. I'll see you both around and about, then." With as confident a grin as he could muster, he inclined his head toward the couple and strode out.

When the door shut behind him, he regretted not further examining the apartment. As he walked across the hallway to his smaller abode, he regretted not making better conversation with the intimidating Mr. Speare. When he entered his room, his son burst out laughing at his scared expression, saying, "Man, you're fucked!"

CHAPTER TWO

❄❄❄❄❄

Jessie had a dream that she was not worthy of waking up until she had experienced a proper dream, something about giant whale tongues and barrels full of rum tumbling on their sides. It seemed a recurring theme, her unworthiness, and thus she couldn't find the willpower to break the stickiness that pressed her legs together and fixed her back to her shirt. With shock, she almost thought she had wet herself. No puddle of urine dampened her bedsheets—chalk another one up for night sweats. Along with strange dreams, she'd been having a lot of those.

She ate eggs for breakfast, as she did nearly every morning, showered without washing her hair, and changed into some presentable clothes. Her pants with the big pockets that hung like kangaroo pouches seemed an appropriate fit for today—she wanted to be all electricity and androgynous bite for her "date" with Angus after school. Paired with her green boots and beanie to combat the cold, she thought she looked pretty confident.

Confident was the opposite of what she truly felt, but pretending was a massive part of the life of an operating depressed girl. Once it got colder or school broke for summer—whichever came first—she figured she'd just remain in bed all day, passionless, sleepy. Her dream hinted that her hormones simply weren't up to the task today. Jessie ignored the ominous signs, shrugged them off as wives' tales. Why she couldn't shrug things off normally was beyond her—but since a boy had actually showed an interest in her, actually wanted her plump lips and small eyes, she felt stronger.

Damn it, she wanted to stand on her own two feet, not get all dependent on some boy! Love shouldn't be like that, not again.

Or so she thought as she took the subway transit to school, listening to an eclectic blend of music with her trusty iPad that matched all the businessy folk on their morning commute. She loved living in the city, sharing the subway, sharing her air with the rest of millions. When her phone vibrated and Angus wished her a good morning, she declined to respond. As much as Jessie, who was actually consciously selfish, loved sharing her life with the city, she wasn't quite ready to share it with him.

Angus was perfect, truly and really. But she wasn't ready. Still, even after explaining her reluctance uncolorfully to him, he insisted on wishing her good evening and good nights and good mornings and maybe a good life. Jessie was flattered: others' wishes had better luck than hers when it came to coming true; at least that's what history had taught her.

She attended class, paid close attention, did her homework during study hall, and hoped to a God she no longer believed in that every action she did that day was good enough. School ended with a reminder by the student council president to stay warm, and a building full of teenagers rushed to the nearest hangouts to partake in a semblance of heat. Jessie took the subway once again, this time closer to the Complexes.

It was on the train when Antony tapped her on her shoulder. She jumped and slapped his hand away, frightened by the sudden touch of a stranger. "Excuse me?" she said, disguising her attitude with a kind voice.

"You're excused," the boy replied with a toothy grin. "If my stalking skills don't deceive me, you live at the Complexes, don't you? Floor E? I'm Antony. I go to the same school and the same apartment building as you. Funny, right?"

Jessie hardly knew what to make of him. She was awkward enough in social situations. Hardly did a stranger take interest in her, nevertheless one of the opposite sex. This must be her lucky year! Or perhaps, on second thought, an unlucky one, if the boy was a true stalker and not just a joker. "Yeah. Not to sound rude or anything but, for someone who shares so much in common with me, I have never seen you before in my life."

"That's what makes it funny," the boy, now named Antony, said. "Coincidences, serendipity, funny, no?" He sniffed at his failure to make a clicking reference. "I tried. But seriously, we do live in the same place. Ask me any question about it, and I am, uh, forty-five percent certain I will know the answer."

After racking her brain for a minute, Jessie grilled him. "What's our landlord's name?"

Antony squinted at her, opened and closed his mouth, ran a hand through his hair, and then proceeded to make noisy, unintelligible sounds that suggested the answer was on the tip of his tongue. "Oh! Oh! I can't tell you her name, but she's got a great big Jewish nose with a horrific mole on it." When Jessie looked unsatisfied, he proffered, "I can tell you our security guard's name, if that'll satisfy you."

"If I believe you, will you lower your voice?"

"Yeah, sure."

"Thanks, Antony." More cordially, Jessie held out her hand. "I'm Jessie Rivera. E02."

The train stopped, spit out a few commuters, and allowed the two to sit down and chat. Antony explained that he lived in E11, thus convincing Jessie of his authenticity. He, only a year her senior, was settling temporarily at the Complexes thanks to his now divorced aunt, Ruthy. Jessie had nearly turned down his offer to hang out when an idea ran through her mind as quickly as a house cat frightened of a fire alarm.

Antony then agreed to being her own personal cockblock during her date with who he guessed was some vile, pimply boy taking advantage of Jessie's kindness. He considered it a gesture of peace between the two of them: he freaked her out a little on the subway, and she drilled him pretty good with the questions validating his identity. Though Jessie suffered muffled conflicted feelings about bringing him, she figured that this particular rendezvous was never officially dubbed a date and that she could tugboat along anyone she pleased. Little

CHAPTER TWO

did Antony know, as they entered the diner named endearingly the Chouette Chouette, that the vile, pimply boy waiting for Jessie was Angus.

The situation was certainly awkward. Jessie sat across from Angus, beside Antony, and fidgeted with her hands inside her kangaroo pockets. No one spoke unless it was to the waitress, who looked bored of receiving unenthusiastic orders from penniless teenagers. Somehow, Jessie figured this situation was all her fault—had she forgotten to say that Angus also lived in floor E, and that Antony might have met him before? Such information seemed vital now. Angus watched her regretfully as she, frustrated, put her hand to her eyes, as if about to cry or scream or fathom something unfathomable.

"Did I," said she, "do something? Or are we all not talking for a reason?"

Angus cleared his throat and attempted to alleviate the tension in his cool voice. "I'm just wondering why you had to bring along somebody when I thought it would be just you and me, you know? It's not like you killed me, but ..." He shrugged.

The waitress returned with their warm cappuccinos and asked if they wanted anything else. Simultaneously, yet in different tones, they all responded with a resounding no. Professionally offended, she left the table to its drama without a look back.

"Okay," Antony said, slowly, "I'll say it. This guy suddenly stomps out while we were hanging out the other day. I don't know why.

COMPLEXES

We were talking, calmly, and then *boom*, he's mad and starts accusing me of brainwashing." He shook his head and looked entreatingly at Jessie. "Maybe you can figure him out, you've known him longer."

Jessie's eyes slid from Antony to Angus. Her eyebrows rose expectantly. The boy who calmly texted her sweet nothings sounded worlds away from the capricious fellow just described.

"It's personal. I just know I'm not getting involved with Antony Shepherd." He stated the name with spit and spite.

"You're not getting involved," Jessie said, already exasperated, "you're just having a cup of coffee with him. Call it what you want, but you don't have to call it a truce. Let's pretend whatever happened that day didn't happen for one hour, will you?" Antony, whose hand covered his mouth as if he were deep in thought, nodded while focusing on the steam rising from his cappuccino. Angus looked as though he were growing increasingly furious, like a raven with ruffled feathers. "For me, Angus?" Jessie reluctantly played her card, and he relented.

The table was then silent. Engulfed in her thoughts, she wondered who cursed her with such luck, why Angus behaved the way he behaved, and why Antony had to show up and ruin a perfectly fine quote-end-quote date. Jessie pointed the blame everywhere while feeling guilty of the true crime: being unable to circumvent this. However, if all she had to endure was bouts of resentment and discomfort, she figured she'd live.

"So … cold for June, isn't it?"

Jessie was relieved that of all kinds of people Antony could have been, he was a mouthy one. "Yeah," she contributed tentatively, "and it only gets worse from here, they say."

"I'm not paying for his coffee," said Angus, rather abruptly. The other two blinked at him as if he were a moving abstract sculpture, and they unable to discern his intentions. "I'll pay for yours, Jess, but not for his. Then we can talk."

"We're already talking, sort of," Antony said, scratching his scalp, "but yeah, I don't really care. She's your sort-of girlfriend after all." He nudged Jessie, knowing full well that while she didn't want to be Angus's girlfriend, he'd appease him by titling her so. "I'm just the cockblock. Now, if you don't mind me, I'm going to call that waitress we so rudely rejected so I can eat me some pancakes."

After Antony ordered his midday meal, the trio (a trio because, all things considered, they were trapped with each other) delved into formally restrained small talk. School, the first thing they had in common, was unsurprisingly the first thing discussed. Jessie and Angus, juniors in high school, voiced their anxiety for the SATs and the college application process. Both aimed high for different though similar reasons—Jessie to prove her worth, and Angus to prove himself against Giles, who, when they moved to the city, transferred to one of the top liberal arts colleges. Antony could not relate, however, as his constant moving around seemed to render learned intelligence useless; he earned a 1700 on his SAT only by sheer luck, and would only use the scores to apply to the closest community college.

"How do you not have goals for yourself?" Jessie asked, almost bewildered by Antony's laid-back demeanor in the face of what she deemed was failure. Half of him was offended by her question, for certainly he had goals; they were just not the academic kind. What he wanted was a wife and kids and a place to live—how he got there seemed, to him, a faraway prospect. She pressed, "But don't you know you can't get a stable home without a good education?"

"Hey, I wanted a place to live, not a 'stable home,' " Antony pointed out. "Big difference."

"So you don't mind being a vagrant," Jessie said, shaking her head in defeat. College, to her, was the be-all end-all. It would define her and her future; her guts yearned and churned for it. Angus, who, on the other hand, was too preoccupied with the present to worry about what the future held for him, cut in saucily, "He's already a vagrant. He and his dad move around a lot."

It wasn't his information to tell, and that offended Antony's other half. Ticked off and showing it through the intensity of his cutting pancakes, he said, "So what if I'm not a guy with huge dreams or with a way to get my little dreams. Doesn't give you a right to judge my goals and my methods. Don't make me call you an elitist, because I will, and it will stick with you for the rest of your perfect little lives." The two stared at him, then stared inward at themselves. Chewing the diner pancakes deliciously dripping with butter and syrup calmed him, but only slightly. "Let's talk about something else, like Miriam's horrific Jewish nose."

"You're willing to call us elitist when you're anti-Semitic!" Angus blurted out.

"Oh, give it a rest, Angus, Miriam is a horrific person in general. The game she plays with the heat is rigged, you know that," agreed Jessie, hurt enough by Antony's tirade to side with him during the new phase of conversation. What he said was true: if she were insulted once, just once, even if it were intrinsically false, it would stick with her. How he knew that it would was beyond her.

Stubborn Angus couldn't overcome his intense dislike for the Antony character. But for Jessie, he'd swallow his pride without giving it more than five thoughts—that was saying something. On a second note, she looked adorable today, in that punky way. He wished he could tell her that. Meanwhile, to please her, he decided to grumble along with the discussion at hand. "It can't be rigged. She decides who gets the heat that day by a raffle. Don't complain, Jess; you actually had it this week."

"Whoa, whoa, whoa, wait," Antony interjected. He and his father were ignorant of the entire raffle setup, and no one had bothered to inform them. Yet another offense by the inhabitants of floor E! He sliced his pancakes roughly and scowled. "When were you going to tell me about the heat thing?"

"I thought my mom told you." The blame rolled off Angus's shoulders with ease. "Anyway, how do you figure it's rigged?"

Jessie admitted after a beat, "I don't know. It'd just be more interesting if it was."

"We should start a riot or something!" Antony passionately recommended.

At the image of the entire floor rioting, Jessie chuckled. "Not a riot, as cool as that would be, but a tally of who gets the heat when. It would make more sense if everyone got the heat at even intervals than through a raffle. Someone could go without heat for months, you feel me?"

"I feel you," Antony passionately reciprocated.

Angus's eyebrow twitched in annoyance. "It's not going to happen." When questioned, he simply repeated himself. "No one on our floor can work together. It just doesn't happen. Someone's going to try to run things, then someone's going to disagree, then we'll try to put it to a vote, then someone's going to get their head lopped off … It's as good as anarchy."

"It's a tally, not a zombie apocalypse," replied Antony, passionately rejecting his scenario.

Angus huffed in response, figuring if someone's head were going to get lopped off, it would be Jonathan's. "I'm exaggerating, obviously. But no one's going to cooperate."

"Why wouldn't they?" Jessie asked, her faith in people's goodness still burning despite her own attempts to become a cynic.

"Because they won't. Maybe it will work for a week or two, but eventually someone will botch up or get lazy or something."

"Is this all hypothetical or are we all serious about this?" Antony had finished his pancakes and was now prepared for some serious conversation. His hand rested on the table, fingers outstretched, as he proposed a different and questionably illegal strategy that was neither contested nor vetoed.

❄❄❄❄❄

Because the heat was in Jonathan's room for the day, he and Giles skipped class to make a dent in the movies. Unfortunately for Jonathan (and perhaps for Giles too), the first movie they selected from the zippered black packet was raw pornography. They exchanged mute glances when the prostitute began "freshening up" in the bathroom, unbuttoning her shirt in a calm, yet subtly sensual manner. "Should we turn this off?" Jonathan asked, disguising his apprehensiveness with a voice glazed over with consideration. Giles responded in the negative, now kicking off his shoes and sitting more comfortably on the couch. The porn continued to play.

The woman, now dressed in classic black lingerie, slipped on sleek heels and walked like a cat out of the bathroom, toward her client. They exchanged a few low words about the experience they were about to share—he liked being dominant, and for the night she would be his girl. The uncharged atmosphere gained voltage once the man began examining her, entreating her to stand on the coffee table and erotically contort her body.

They had just begun kissing, hands in hair, hands on the chest, hands cupping necks, when Jonathan paused the movie. The couple froze on a disgusting frame in which their mouths were connected only by a bridge of tongue. "I don't think I can watch this," he said honestly.

"Not into this kind of stuff?" Giles said, purposefully dumb to his true intentions. Jonathan stammered, his tongue hammering in his mouth. "Or are you just not into it with me in the room?"

"Yeah—no—sort of." He slapped the palms of his hands to his cheeks, his calming gesture. The question was asked for two reasons: the ice and the water, the surface and the core. To follow Giles's lead, Jonathan was to answer both truthfully. At least, that's how he interpreted his oddly worded queries. "I'm not certain," he began, selecting his words with caution, "that we're at this level where we can watch this together." Jonathan's eyes met Giles's, who unflinchingly gazed back.

Raising his index finger, and then raising his middle finger to make a pair, Giles replied,

CHAPTER TWO

"If one party is not certain, what if the other party is?"

"That depends on the situation."

"What other situation is there other than the present?" Third, fourth, fifth fingers were raised, curiously, until he dropped his hand and returned his attention to the grotesque form of human affection displayed on the screen. Jonathan, on the other hand, was slightly lost in the course of the conversation. He found his way, as he always did, through Giles's eyes, directed solemnly at the man and the prostitute. "I had sex with her," he added plainly, an impure fact.

Jonathan swallowed. "I know." With that, he knew he had lost, and that they were at that porn-watching level. He pressed play, and the TV moaned.

In the early days of their friendship, Giles insisted that he lose his virginity. He had neither reason nor rhyme to his sudden urge. Jonathan took him out to a variety of bars, watched him flirt and kiss, but Giles could not act on the impulse to go to bed with these strangers. Every night he began with a positive vibe, as if this was the night. For Jonathan's time and effort, he offered an arm around the shoulder, a sign of intimacy rarely obtained. They'd stride to their first watering hole and search for the stealthy gems of bar-goers that piqued Giles's interest.

"Join me," he'd say in a low voice to the object of his affections for the night the instant they were unaccompanied, "I feel a little lost." Jonathan drank while they shared a cigarette outside, talking of strangely intimate things, like how beautifully right the world feels when one sees birds flying in a perfect V. He imagined that Giles unconsciously prepared a response to everything, and that he initiated more serious chats matter-of-factly, as if he breathed profundity. Then, they would return, walking slightly closer to one another, Giles sometimes brushing the waist or shoulder with his uncallused fingers. If the person had come with a group, occasionally Giles was successful at prying his object away with the subtlety of a con artist, and they would advance to a club, where they danced their drinks away.

When he kissed, he wrapped his fingers at the hairline, entwined his index finger in the hair, and pressed his thumb to the ear. Hips and lips pressed together in the center of a dance floor, Jonathan had almost mistaken Giles and his object as a couple. During passionate nights they'd locate an alleyway or a bathroom stall, supposedly to do their business, but he always returned to Jonathan more drunk than the last time, asking to go home.

The first night, Giles slept on the bed, and Jonathan, on the couch. The second night, though they agreed to alternate, Giles approached Jonathan on the bed and lay beside him, muttering incoherently. Back then, they were strangers, sharing a bed, one gay, and one halfway out of the closet—but did it matter? Jonathan counted lambs until he slept, palms clammy.

CHAPTER TWO

He thought he was doing Giles a favor when he introduced him to Roonie. The now desperate Giles drank enough to throw up on sidewalks, and gravely chain-smoked his hangovers away. Although Jonathan couldn't fathom why losing his virginity was so important to him, he felt it was his duty as his— mentor?—to assist him in his endeavor. "Look, I know a prostitute," he said, watching Giles's impassive expression, expecting a change, "She owes me a favor. Maybe I can set you up with her at a discount." Giles's head pivoted on his neck, craned upward, craned downward, eyes smoldering with an unknown emotion, like his cigarette butts in the ashtray.

Roonie agreed to do it, and Giles paid her named price. Both young men were in E07 when she knocked and entered, her black hair in a formal bun and long slits in her maxi skirt. "Boys," she said, memorably, "as fun as it would be, I don't think I'm fucking the both of you." At that, Jonathan reluctantly excused himself, planning to smoke his whole pack outside while he waited. As he closed the door, he saw Giles looking meaningfully at him.

Jonathan spent his entire exile endeavoring to name the emotion paired with that look—anger, perhaps? Anxiety? He would see that face in his sleep, furrowed eyebrows and narrow eyes and all. After going through half his cigarette pack, Jonathan gave a sweeping look at the Complexes, where his new accomplice was having sex with a prostitute, and decided to go get something to eat to quiet his stirring stomach. Stirring, because he was

76

beginning to really love Giles, and if he were that prostitute he would make love to him for free and forever.

"Roonie left," said the text that ordered him to return to his apartment. Enough time had passed that Jonathan guessed they really had done it. Wondering what words would be exchanged, he took the stairs, two at a time, instead of the excruciatingly sluggish elevator. When he unlocked the door, Giles was pouring brandy—the kind that they drank when they wanted to act like adults. "It is done," he said, in an almost holy tone.

They drank a lot that night. With his filter swept away by the alcohol, Jonathan had to ask: "How was it?" He knew Giles would respond with either one sentence or a plethora of unwanted detail. He hoped for the former.

Swallowing his drink, he responded in a manner typical of those who had just had sex, yet unusual for him. "Not what I expected." Also abnormally, he disclosed an appropriate amount of detail. "I didn't want to kiss her. Maybe that was it."

"Maybe. You lose some of the intimacy that way."

They stumbled to bed, and lay close enough to smell the alcohol on each other's breath. "Hmm," Giles said thoughtfully, "Maybe …"

"What?" Drunkenness and exhaustion tugged Jonathan's eyelids down.

CHAPTER TWO

In the morning, he knew Giles took too long to reply on purpose. The moment was gone, and so was he.

COMPLEXES

Chapter Three

When perusing Angus's book of firsts, those with perceptive eyes would easily notice that Giles was involved in every one of them, from his first laugh to his first walk. Thus, it was easy for Angus to create for himself a dependent complex—he could not achieve much without his dear older brother. His admiration for Giles shone on his skin; his hate clenched the fibers of his heart. Those two emotions switched places when Giles left. Angus hated nearly everything now.

If he hated the idea of a sit-in, he didn't show it. So he prepared for the protest—he urinated, binge-ate, and stretched out his legs. His mother only gave him a bemused look and a kiss on the forehead as he left, bounding down the stairs to the boiler room, where the central heat was controlled. Jessie and Antony were already there, sitting with their backs to the door.

"I've made a list of our demands," Antony said, waving around a scrap of college-ruled paper. "An organized and even distribution of heat. And … that's it. I guess I shouldn't have made 'demands' plural."

Jessie laughed. Angus scoffed, but played along. It was early in the morning yet—Miriam Bickel had to eventually come around to adjust the heat. In the meantime, the three talked sparsely. Angus remained wary of Antony, for he was always wary of people unlike those he was used to. Antony was the type he generally avoided for the same reason opticians suggest people avoid looking directly at the sun. Angus didn't want sunniness. He was perfectly comfortable in his newfound cloud of gloom, thank you very much.

It hardly struck him that, in previous points in his life, Angus was that sunny person. Giles clung to him like a newly inked tattoo precisely for the joy and brightness he provided. With that tattoo ripped off, taking layers of flesh with it, Angus was only a wounded animal, bent on revenge.

In that way, Antony was a reminder of what he could have been.

"Shh! Here she comes," whispered Antony, eyes wide and excited. Slow-paced footsteps on the creaky stairs grew louder. As Miriam turned the bend, her face contorted in pure annoyance at the sight of three human boulders plopped conveniently in her way.

"We're protesting," Antony, the obvious spokesperson, explained when she tensely asked what the hell was going on. "We'll sit here until our demand is met. We want an organized and even distribution of heat."

Miriam laughed. As the oppressor, she sounded quite evil to the sitting trio.

"Don't be ridiculous. Get out of the way, I've got work to do."

Angus hated being considered petty. "Lady, you obviously don't know how this works. We don't budge until you budge."

"Fine," she crowed, "the heat's in E10 anyway. I'm sure Mrs. Schmidt will be grateful!" She blurted a loud *"ha!"* and exited. In Angus's twisted imagination, she flew up the stairs on a broomstick while her amused cackle resounded off the walls and stairs.

Jessie and Angus simultaneously shot Antony despondent looks, both of which rolled off his back like a dribble of sweat. "So we sit in for a little longer, no big deal," he said, leaning back against the boiler room door nonchalantly. "Don't tell me you're bored already, Gus?"

With more lethality, he retorted, "Don't you dare call me that."

"Okay, okay. Angus." Antony raised his palms, acknowledging that he'd danced over another mine in the field.

In response, Angus scoffed, shaking his head in irritated disbelief. Why he voluntarily chose to spend more time with Antony Shepherd was beyond him. He didn't like how prying he was. He hated how he tried to tempt him with friendship and cigarettes and booze. What's more, Antony acted as though none of his actions were offensive in the slightest. Didn't he know—?

CHAPTER THREE

Realistically, Angus relented, he didn't know. No one outside of the Speare family knew how they were falling apart, crumbing like a brick-walled building against the erosion of time and weather. And it hurt. It hurt that his family, the only people he truly loved, the only folks he trusted and talked to, had lost its ability to speak. Everyone—even Giles, Angus figured—was muted by a twisted shame whose roots grew in pride.

Even though Angus spent another six hours numbing his behind against the cold concrete with Jessie and Antony, he remained quiet. They exchanged small talk and numbers and anecdotes of warmer days, but he clung to his secrets, just as Jessie and Antony clung to theirs.

He figured they didn't need to know anyway.

Gerard scored a job as an auto salesman on the fringes of the city, but he hadn't a clue how to celebrate his achievement. Money was tight, but he felt the need to congratulate himself in some way, or else he'd tumble into an upsetting lethargy he associated with his depressing twenties, when he lived off the couches of generous craigslist users in exchange for cleaning the house or something equally simple. People took pity on him, a single dad with a noisy baby. When Antony grew older, however, hearts hardened: two vagrant men, despite one's being a teenager, only looked like laziness.

Was it laziness on his part? Gerard heard of success stories of single moms braving college while simultaneously caring for their kids with the help of their parents. Had he and his parents been on speaking terms, he might have joined that army of heroines. So he blamed himself, constantly, for being unable to provide for Antony. He blamed himself for stealing his father's Rolex watch and his mother's precious diamonds to purchase heroin. He even blamed himself for considering abandoning Antony in a cramped, messy apartment.

Maybe he did too much blaming and not enough work. But Gerard simply had no clue what he was destined to do in life. Internally, he knew he was no businessman or artist, certainly not a mathematician or scientist. If anything, he learned from Alice that he was a lover. He easily loved Alice, loved Antony, loved beauty, loved ugliness. Gerard could find something to love in nearly everything—and following that destiny, to find his ultimate love, led him here, where he met Mara.

Mara, as far as Gerard knew, was Alice's dramatic foil, what Alice should have become but never could be. She was as courteous as Alice was coarse; she was as family-oriented as Alice was free-spirited. Alice's hair resembled daytime, while

CHAPTER THREE

Mara's reflected sleek evening, the shine where the light hit representing the stars. Gerard flushed at images of her thin arms, bony elbows, and small yet mature breasts underneath her neutral-colored cardigans. The more he heard of her the more he liked her, perhaps loved her.

She just had to be married to the most frightening man in the building. James reminded him of Holbein's painting, *Henry VIII*, the English king, in both appearance and character, even though he knew little to nothing of him. When he entered their apartment last night, he half expected him to scold innocent Mara for bringing a stranger inside. Gerard feared what he did to her—probably monstrous things, such as forcing her to wash the dishes and mar her hands every night without a please or a thank you.

Knowing his opponent did not make things easier on Gerard's mind. Though he imagined James as a perfect fiend, he still could not bring himself to make the right advances for fear of becoming a home wrecker in an apartment where two young men (intimidating, yet human) also lived. He did not relish the idea of causing family drama, the kind consistently represented on cheesy soap operas. And yet he must do something to inform Mara of his affections.

A letter was the most appropriate thing he could think of. The very thought made him sick to his stomach, as it reminded him of his teenage years when love letters were more commonplace. It was the most appropriate idea, and yet, it was juvenile, ridiculous. A man tells a woman he loves her straightforwardly—another lesson Alice had rightfully taught him.

Gerard, now at home, slid his hands down his face, dragging his cheeks down unattractively. What was he to do? Nothing? The very concept instilled restlessness within him, as if his heart had a buzzer slapped on it with Velcro.

While contemplating his next steps, Gerard heard a heavy hand knock on his door. Jolted by the sudden noise, he opened it to find his surly landlord on his figurative welcome mat. "Mrs. Bickel," he began, scrambling to regain his composure after the surprise. "It's nice to see you."

"Your son," she said, with a long fingernail pointing at Gerard's nose. "Get him out of my way or so help me God—"

He found his face buried in his palm in exasperation. "Of course. Antony. What did he do?"

"Young Mr. Shepherd thinks it's cute to protest how I run things. Get down to the boiler room and talk him out of his childish tantrums. Well? Go!" Miriam stomped down the hallway of floor E and knocked on someone else's door, presumably to complain and point fingers again. Not wanting to incite her wrath, Gerard hurried down the steps to the boiler room, where he found three adolescents, Antony among them, half-asleep, in awkward positions on the floor.

With a hand on his forehead and another on his hip, Gerard shook his head and yelled with force, "Wake up, kids!" Each one jumped three inches off the floor before rubbing their eyes and noticing Gerard's presence. He knelt down to their level, not disguising the disappointment on his face. "Antony, what are you doing? You've gone and pissed off our landlord—again—and I can't have it this time, you know."

"In my defense, our last landlord's daughter hit on me first," the stubborn half-wit of a son mumbled.

The Asian girl sitting beside Antony responded with as much sense as the situation would allow: "We're protesting the heat raffle." With halfhearted, bored enthusiasm, she explained the heating situation, then prodded at Antony, thus shoving the blame for their sore derrieres on him.

Quick footsteps echoed their way down to the boiler room. As they grew louder, Gerard whispered quickly, "As much as I'd like to applaud you for your fair spirit, son, we really can't afford to piss anyone off this time. So get up off your ass and come upstairs with me before Miriam—"

The footsteps stopped. Gerard stood and pivoted to see Mara Speare and another woman who was presumably the girl's mother. Only after he recovered from his surprise at the object of his affection's presence did he realize he'd completely ignored the third kid participating in the protest—Angus Speare. Mara gazed down at her son, eyes neutral, hand covering her mouth, concealing an amused smile or disappointed frown.

At the sight of his mother, Angus stood up and stretched his back. "We didn't think this through," he said to his now ex-comrades in protest. "We have school tomorrow."

"Aw, man, you're gonna ditch because of school? Where's your spirit? What about you, Jessie?"

With a glance at her own mother, who gestured for her to go, Jessie jumped ship. "I'm sorry, Antony," she said earnestly, "but I've had to pee since noon." With that, she scuttled up the stairs.

"Come on!" Antony yelled, looking back and forth between Angus and the place where Jessie once sat. Unsympathetic, Angus shrugged and followed his mother like an obedient duckling.

Entertained but exasperated, Gerard extended a hand to his son. "Doesn't your butt hurt?"

A flame in his son's eye flickered, but he grasped Gerard's hand and groaned as he stood. "Excuse me, but my butt is made of oak." He paused, then added, "I take that back, that just sounded weird."

They laughed, and Gerard lightly patted the back of his son's head. "Come on, kiddo." Halfway up the stairs, he confessed, "I'm glad you're making friends, regardless."

"Do you think we'll stay here long?"

There it was, the inevitable question, said in the same neutral tone. Gerard wondered what his son gained by asking such a thing. Did he plan ahead depending on the answer, remaining distant as to not disappoint any new friendships? Or was it his way of asking permission to get more comfortable? No matter—Gerard hardly knew the answer. "For as long as we can afford it, I think," he said truthfully. "Until Ruthy decides she doesn't need us to give her support."

"What support are we giving her?" Antony took each step behind his father deliberately. Gerard imagined his eyes, perhaps a little hurt, with more ocean than his usual flame gusto. "If anything, she's supporting us."

He paused, considering the question, then decided to settle with the obvious. "She just needs family around, that's all."

Antony stopped, gazing out a convenient window into the high skyline. "I want to go back to the West Coast, Dad. Isn't it warmer down in San Diego? Let's go there."

Thinking of Mara, Gerard shook his head. "I don't know. It's a long way to San Diego. We'll see. Don't you like it here? You just made a couple of friends."

COMPLEXES

"I'm just tired of the cold." Antony climbed a couple more stairs, surpassing his father by a few steps.

Gerard stared at his son's back, his suddenly broad shoulders, and the wrinkles on his white shirt. "I am, too, son."

She had fallen asleep to reading Mary Shelley while simultaneously avoiding the world. Her dreams were empty, but they caused her to sweat. Drawers closed with a bang, awakening her, though not stirring her. Five minutes of more thumping and incoherent grumbling finally convinced Mara to move from her comfortable nest of pillows on the couch. Only after readjusting her now messy braid in the mirror did she confront the ruckus, which originated from Giles's room.

"Giles?" she called, knocking politely.

It was James, home two hours early from work. "Come in, Mara." The door creaked open, revealing garbage bags half-filled with, and drawers half-empty of, clothes. Other goods belonging to Giles were shoved haphazardly into a large cardboard box, and the bedding was crumpled on the ground. In the center of this mayhem stood James, who appeared to be breathing heavily, looking directly at his wife as if he'd been caught red-handed.

CHAPTER THREE

"You're not disowning the boy, are you?" Mara demanded, her voice fringing upon shrill.

"You haven't seen what I've seen," James said, as if that justified his behavior. "He doesn't deserve to live under my roof anymore." He returned to packing, not bothering to fold the clothes neatly or arrange the items in a more appropriate manner. There went the CD case with the graduation card hidden inside, the photos of his First Communion.

Mara watched, too bewildered to stop him. "I might have not," she began, gathering her strength to oppose her husband, "but do you think I don't know what you know? Do you think me that naïve?" Crossing her arms, she widened her stance to block the doorway, prepared to stop James if he attempted to exit. "I know our son is gay or bisexual or not the way you want him to be, but he's still our son."

"Still our son?" rumbled James. "Still our son after carousing about with that redheaded devil next door? After taking advantage of our kindness for months and yet not returning home? I don't know what's gotten into him, Mara. You should see the way he looks at me, the way he looks at our door when he passes by."

Although she felt him and understood him, she couldn't allow her son to be so casually kicked out of the family. Even if Giles did harbor such hatred for his family, Mara still loved him dearly.

COMPLEXES

Responding with poisoned revenge fixed nothing, even if part of her wished to join James. "Giles never said he hated us. It's all in your mind. He's just going through a phase right now, a rebellious phase. He'll come back, just give him more time." Frightened, and yet soothed by her own words, Mara approached him like one would a scared, wild dog. Her outstretched hand now rested on James's shoulder—he shrugged her away.

"How much time have we already given him? Months? Almost a year now?"

"He's our son. He deserves all the time in the world."

James's glance shifted toward the small window, currently providing the only light into the room. If he were to open it, the air would smell like impending snow. "He could have all the time in the world and still not make a decision," James concluded harshly, yet gravely. "I'm going to speak to the boy, the next time I see him. Try to talk some sense into him."

Cautiously, Mara asked for clarification. "What do you mean by 'sense'? Bullying him will get you nowhere, James; Giles is much smarter than that."

"Who said I was going to bully him?" James said stubbornly. "We'll just have a little talk, he and I."

From the apartment's entrance came the shuffling of the doorknob. Angus was home. Mara stepped back from James, gave

CHAPTER THREE

the overturned room one last sweeping look, and joined Angus, whose hand was already engulfed in the container full of cookies, in the kitchen. After welcoming him home, she proceeded to read *Frankenstein* without turning any pages. It was not, in the end, James she was worried about—he'd been aggressive from the very beginning, from his proposal to their moving from Australia. It was Giles who occupied her worries with his strange behavior and mysterious double meanings. Always something of a bizarre child, he used to be the glue that kept the family together—kept Angus from feeling James's rage, kept James from overwhelming Mara, kept Mara from spoiling Angus.

They were falling apart without him. Her husband's anger and threatening spirit reached all ends of the small family. Mara was more fretful than ever, subdued by James into silence. Angus had matured from a sweet boy to an ever angry young man with a fire in his throat. Finally, everyone blamed Giles for it all.

Angus spat a cookie out into the garbage can. "They taste horrible stale," he commented to no one in particular.

"Eat them when they're fresh, then," Mara advised, smiling through her peevishness.

"You make way too many," he continued. "I think I'm gaining weight."

Raising her eyes from the book, she observed her son's very lanky frame. She was waiting for the time when he would grow into his height, like Giles had in his senior year. "It wouldn't hurt to gain a little." At that, Angus looked at her reproachfully. She then avoided his gaze, returning vacantly to her book. "I won't make any more if you don't want them."

"I never said I didn't want them, Mom."

The words trickled from her mouth, like blood from an internal wound. "No one eats them nowadays, anyway."

"I do, when they're fresh," he argued.

She pursed her lips to prevent more fallout, imagining the ecstatic look on Giles's face when chocolate chip cookies burst forth from the oven's warm womb. He'd been a rabid eater in his formative years; Angus, not so much in comparison, even today.

"Whatever, Mom. I know you're upset, but you don't have to take it out on me." With that, Angus shut the cookies' container with a resounding *plip!* and stomped back out of the apartment, destination unknown.

With no one left to kid, Mara shut her book and shut her eyes again. James was still rummaging in Giles's room. "James," her voice pealed like a bell that no one heeded, "you're not going to find anything new there."

He finally exited, wiping his hands together as if he were just dealing with something dirty. "It's all cleaned up," he said, indicating the room. "He can choose whether to grab his stuff and go or unpack." He settled on the couch beside Mara, even though both knew they had nothing to say to each other.

Their relationship milestones were becoming increasingly depressing by the day. The last time they had gone out as a couple was three and a half years ago. The last time they had kissed was three years ago. The last time they had made love was four years ago. She couldn't remember the last time he had looked at her with love.

The days they had spent together in Calcutta felt worlds away. They met in a slum, he a grand man lost while on a tour of the country, she a self-made merchant of arbitrary goods salvaged from various dumps. "Each *taka* goes to me getting out of here," she proclaimed to each customer, as if it would endear them to her. She remembered selling cheese by the slice, peanut butter and cumin by the scoop. To every new face, she'd explain her mission with great enthusiasm, until her customer felt the same passion as she did.

"I want to do something wonderful with my life now," a man said in broken Bengali when he knocked on her window and received her life story in return. Only then did she squint through her dirtied screen and take a good look at him, a handsome white man with broad shoulders and arms that filled his jacket's sleeves.

COMPLEXES

"How much is it for a small map?" he struggled to ask, scanning her wares.

Finally putting her school-taught English to good use, Mara said, "No map. Where do you try to go?"

Relieved to find an English-speaking person, he said with an accent that sounded vaguely British to her, "Victoria Memorial. I got lost, or more like, sidetracked, in the—the uh, Jadubabur Bazaar, and—"

"Slow down, English man, I cannot understand you." Years out of school had rusted her comprehension, and the man's handsomeness, though unconventional and slightly on the bulky side, distracted her. "You were lost in the bazaar and you want to go to Victoria Memorial, yes?" She jumped from her cross-legged position on her stool and flipped her makeshift sign from "Open" to "Closed" and accompanied him for quite a distance to the memorial.

Along the way, James—that was the well-dressed man's name—felt obligated to explain that he wasn't English, but Australian. He was in Bangladesh on a trip with his family, who was determined to visit as many major cities in the world as possible while being entirely cultured about it. "That means learning as much of the language you can a month before the trip," James sheepishly said, pacing his words carefully, "but it is worth it when you can order food at restaurants without looking silly." Mara laughed, feeling that looking silly the smallest worry a man could have in the world.

They talked and walked about two kilometers, he telling of the many lands he visited in his youth, she of Calcutta and the many people she'd encountered, from old women to lost men. "Not many English-speaking people dare knock on my window," she said, "They are afraid of the dirty, thin, brown-skinned woman behind the counter."

"Why would they be afraid of you?"

"They are afraid," she explained sadly, "of the poverty here."

Although James had already insinuated it, he told her that he was very well-off financially, and that his parents made a practice of these trips mostly for philanthropic reasons. "I own a resort, you might have heard of it." She hadn't. Australia, to her, was a fanciful land of animal trainers and kangaroos.

"Isn't it strange how big the world is?" she remarked when he listed the places he'd visited, from Paris to Dubai, from Dublin to Tokyo. Travelling and embracing new cultures were second nature to him, since he began doing so at a very young age. Languages came easily, and the various concepts of respect struck him as incredibly important. James even related his mother's bizarre predicament of almost giving birth to him in Los Angeles, which would have effectively made him a United States citizen. With all that moving around, Mara had to wonder if he was exhausted of it.

COMPLEXES

Mara had lived in Calcutta all her life. She lived the unexceptional life of a girl in desolation, with elderly parents and younger siblings to feed. "I once was taken care of, and now I must take care of them," she elucidated dutifully. "Now my younger brothers are older. They are beginning to feed the family themselves. I have lived on my own for a year. I am trying to buy a ticket to Italy."

"Why Italy?"

Although she avoided his gaze, embarrassed, her eyes twinkled like a Christmas tree. "I forget the word for it, but great art, Mr. James, great art is there." He proffered the word, "Renaissance," and she was mortified to admit that he was correct, as if she hadn't expected it to be common knowledge. She painted a vivid memory of her as a child, stealing art history books from the library to marvel at Michelangelo's Hellenistic nudes, the early figures of Masaccio, da Vinci's mysterious sketches. "It is very different than the art in India," she said, attempting to explain her wonder. "It is"—she sighed—"almost perfect."

They arrived shortly at Victoria Memorial, a marble palace erected and clearly named by the English. "This is where we part," Mara said with the awkward poise of a college tour guide. "It has been ... good." They shook hands; she felt his strong grip against her rough skin.

CHAPTER THREE

She was a quarter down the road to her shop when James seized her shoulder, pivoting her around like a gauche ballerina. Breathlessly, he said, "Let me take you to Italy."

And, without a second thought to it, she agreed.

The cat died in its sleep again, and Giles woke up to the dull smell of cigarettes. Jonathan still lay asleep beside him, his red hair tousled like a child's. He sniffed and groaned, feeling congested and terrible and hungover, although he'd consumed no alcohol last night. Sitting on the bed, he burned his throat with another cigarette, swallowing the coal-like smoke and exhaling it from his nose.

He figured that whenever the cat died and he saw Angus's tearstained, dirty face, he would wake up again. Lovingly and ironically, he'd named it Finch, after Atticus Finch, one of his favorite literary characters during his tenth year. Finch, discovered as an old cat, only survived a year in the Speare household. He died, underneath the shade of a rubber tree, on the kitchen floor. Giles found him first, nudged him gingerly with his toe before confirming that the cat wasn't breathing. Angus was informed in Giles's usual blunt manner—there was no better way to relay a death, after all.

COMPLEXES

His little brother cried for hours, holding the limp fur as close as he would if it were alive. "Let's bury him, please," Angus begged, and even though Giles had homework and reading to do, he agreed. They dragged the shovel into the spacious lawn, selected an appropriate spot, tied together a cross with sticks, and took turns shoveling.

As they devoted Finch's body to the earth, Giles pondered the phenomenon. Death. Was this it, this anticlimactic pile of bones and skin? Closed green eyes and bent whiskers? Though children's stories and plays endeavored to convince him that death was a blue fire, a hooded man, a lustful woman in a black dress, he forever remembered it as Finch, the gray old cat with green eyes and buoyant paws that often startled him awake during godless hours.

His second cigarette collapsed into ash when Jonathan squirmed awake. "Jesus, you're like an alarm clock, Giles," he said, rubbing his glassy eyes. "Always up with the cock, huh?"

"Don't be cheeky," Giles replied half tetchily, half fondly.

"Aye-aye, captain." He turned over and returned to sleep. If only it were that easy.

A feeling of foreboding had been frequenting Giles's mind as of late. Coupled with that dream, it left him curiously nervous in his toes and fingertips, as if he needed to pace, as if he needed something to toy with. He appeased this bodily anxiety this morning by washing his face, thoroughly, pressing his fingers to the fold of his nose, experimentally squashing the bags underneath his eyes. Soap clung onto his hairline, water dripped from his slowly blinking eyelids. He examined himself, looking for his pupils in his dark brown eyes, while gripping the sink with his antsy hands.

Someone knocked on the door, and his attention snapped like a snake's to the source of the noise. Wiping his moist mouth with the back of his hand, Giles approached the door and looked through the peephole.

"Who is it?" Jonathan asked, his voice muffled by pillows.

"No one," Giles said after confirming that it was his father.

"Mmf, sleep," he then grumbled, turning over in bed and, Giles guessed, falling asleep for the second time this morning.

When Giles opened the door, he found himself looking slightly down to make eye contact with James. This or the very sight of his prodigal son caused irritability in James, as his eyes narrowed and his breath noticeably held. Giles suddenly felt quite vulnerable with his bare chest exposed to the cold and strands of his now long hair plastered to his forehead as compared to James, who was dressed professionally for work. Both wanted to say something, but neither could find the appropriate words. A simple good morning would not suffice as a temporary bridge between warring minds, but Giles said it anyway, with as civil a tone as he could manage.

"Is that all you have to say?" James said, clearly dissatisfied with Giles's choice of salutation. In context, perhaps it was disrespectful. "I've come to talk to you. It's urgent."

Turning his neck, Giles glanced at Jonathan, who lay asleep in the ruffled bed. James looked in that direction also, with a very disgusted scowl. "He's asleep," he assured his father. "Say what you must."

"All your things are packed," James stated, pointing down the hallway. "Save us the pain and disappointment and leave, fully, or return, forget the boy, and we will forget about all of this." His finger remained pointed in the direction of home, a word Giles no longer associated with E01.

In his father's voice, Giles could hear no mercy behind the front of retribution and spite. He had wanted to avoid making this decision for as long as possible, but the day of reckoning had come. "I can't return home," he responded. "Not after what you've done."

"I've done nothing, nothing to offend this family. Look at yourself, *son.*" His hands twitched, grappling internally with the urge to become angry fists. "Look at what you've done to me, to your mother."

Giles raised his chin, instinctually asserting his height. "Oh," he said, "now, of all times, you care about Mom."

"What do you mean by that, boy?" said James threateningly.

"Don't play dumb with me. I know you cheated on her. With all due respect, I could kill you for what you've done, Father. But I'm trying to help you instead. If you want your son back, which I know you do, trace your footsteps back to where it all went wrong."

He slammed the door on James's intrusive foot. "You don't understand," he insisted.

Giles glared at him, dangerous. "You're almost pathetic." The gap between the door and the wall closed, resoundingly. He resisted the urge to check the peephole for the direction James, who didn't knock again, decided to go. "Nathan," he then called, massaging his closed eyelids, "I know you heard everything." The mass of bedsheets didn't stir. With a sigh, Giles collapsed onto the bed beside him again, facedown, hand on the small of Jonathan's back, as if he were helping him walk uphill.

Angus and Jessie, along with many other high school students, tacitly agreed to go home instead of celebrating the end of the school year at one of their regular haunts. They walked to the subway together, not saying much. Not that Angus minded— the obligation to talk often wore him out, so he liked their silences, and pretended that they were meaningful and full of love.

He first met Jessie a few days after he moved to the Complexes and transferred into the same school. She sat beside him in English class, and had dyed hair that brushed her shoulders, its black roots starting to grow in. To be perfectly honest, Angus had hardly noticed her until she cut her hair into a stylish pixie that reminded him of his mother's hair when he was a five-year-old, when times were simpler and happier. Then he started to take more note of her profile than the class: her slight under-bite, her plump lips, and how her eyes squinted at the whiteboard as if she couldn't see.

"Do you need glasses or something?" were the first words Angus spoke to her, in a low whisper during class.

Her shoulders shifted into a shrug. "I have them; I just never wear them." She looked back at him curiously, obviously wondering why the quiet new student took interest in her squinting habits. "I look stupid in glasses," she admitted.

"I'm sure you wouldn't look stupid," Angus kindly remarked.

Their conversation, though cut short by the teacher's asking for the students' attention, continued as if uninterrupted a week later, in hushed voices behind the teacher's back. "I look like a nerd in glasses," Jessie confessed. "As if I weren't enough of one already!"

"You're not a nerd."

"Oh really?" she challenged. "I like weird music and weird television shows and weird books. I'd say that I'm a nerd."

With a concealed laugh, Angus replied, "You've only proved that you're weird, not that you're a nerd."

The teacher called Angus out on his talking, thus asking him to give his thoughts on Oedipus's unfortunate tragedy. Jessie stifled her giggles when all Angus had to contribute was, "His mom was an unfortunate MILF."

And in this manner they talked, brushing past each other in English class until sophomore year ended. Angus's excuse for asking for her number was, "Let's keep in touch over the summer." By that time, Jessie's hair had gotten even shorter, and their relationship a tad warmer.

Once or twice a week they regularly texted each other; it was only fitting that over text in the middle of junior year Angus confessed his growing attachment to her. "You're really an amazing girl—I really like you."

"Like, like like?"

"I guess you can say it that way."

"I'm not looking for a relationship right now, sorry."

COMPLEXES

Despite the heavy gravity crushing his heart to the ground, Angus persisted. "Can we still be friends?"

"Of course."

From then on, Angus did little to mask his feelings for her. Jessie didn't seem to mind his advances, his sweet wishes good night and good morning, although she never reciprocated. She was, however, unendingly and visibly thankful for his friendship. In that way, Angus still felt valued.

Still, Jessie grew quieter and quieter by the week. Angus, who mistook her silence for comfort and tranquility, didn't know that she often felt like she ran out of interesting things to say. So whenever they did hang out, Angus would bait her with incentives to talk until something put that glow in her dark eyes. Sometimes she would leave him alone prematurely, saying she was tired or needed sleep. Despite his fear that she was entirely uninterested in him, Angus pursued her anyway.

"Do you want to hang out with Antony?"

The question, like a light pat on the cheek, broke the silence on the otherwise mumbling subway. Jessie looked up at him expectantly, phone in her gloved hand, prepared to respond to a text message. "Do we have to?" Angus complained. Not only did he have a bad impression of Antony, but he also found that Antony persistently got in between him and Jessie.

CHAPTER THREE

After briefly considering his complaint, Jessie replied, "The more the merrier, yes?"

Angus, off-put by her insistence, scowled. "Do you like him?"

Jessie's eyebrow cocked in confusion. "Like, like like?" Angus nodded. "No, of course not," she responded with a little laughing exhale. She shot him a quizzical, slightly teasing look. "Are you jealous?"

The train doors opened; Jessie and Angus joined the shuffle of commuters up the dank stairs into the cold air. Simply pretending not to hear the question worked in Angus's favor, as Jessie didn't pursue the conversation. His wounded expression was enough to answer.

Before they could board the elevator, Antony's voice rang down the entrance hall. "Hey, guys, in here!" he called, head poking out of the security doorway. Other than exchanging guarded looks, they obeyed his beckoning and met Sans for the first time.

"A member of the Speare family, in the flesh! Pleased to meet you, son, pleased to meet you. I was wondering when, in this past year, would one of you drop by and say hi to little old me in the security room. I meet everyone in person at least once—ah, Ms. Rivera, also a pleasure, also a pleasure. I had the opportunity to say hi to your mother one day, chirpy woman, she is, very nice, very nice. But like I was saying, I know everyone in these here Complexes, but nothing's better than hearing a person's

COMPLEXES

story from his own mouth. A few years ago, a fellow lived over in E11, where you do now, Antony, and he was a real sweetie. You see, he wanted to start a band, so he'd play his chords on his acoustic guitar down in this here room, in this here room! Penniless as a pauper, he was, and too stubborn to do anything he didn't love. So he spent all day here with me, writing songs about his life, about all the girls that shunned his pale ass, even a song about his mother's boyfriends. That was a real tearjerker; I'd ask him to sing it at the end of every day. Now what did he call it? No Comely. Some reference to another song, by some nineties band only strange kids like him listen to, no doubt, no doubt. I told him that he don't need other people or a band or anything, that he could make simple songs out of his acoustic guitar, but he didn't seem to dig that that much. And I told him that he ought to go outside, play for coins in the case, but he refused because he tried before, and no one liked his music, and he didn't really want to play Beatles songs on the street because that's just not his style, not the Beatles, although you really would never have guessed, 'cause he sported this bowl cut like the Beatles and played left handed like McCartney! Maybe he was just bad at what he did and I was ashamed to tell him, but that one song was real sad, cross my heart it was, promise it was. It should have been a hit, but you know the radio nowadays, repeating the same five songs over and over again and no one else but me gets tired of it! Brainwashed by alien dubstep, is what I call it. Back to the guy. Yeah, he got kicked out of the Complexes, and he made this real funny joke saying that he wasn't complex enough to live here. Not funny? Yeah, you had to be there, you had to be there. I wish that guy well, I really do wish that guy well."

Sans paused, stroking his great black beard, deep in thought. "You look like you got something to say, Mr. Speare." he finally said, his eyes twinkling right at Angus. "Tell me something, tell me a story, yeah, a story. I promise I won't interrupt; I'm a good listener like that. Antony over here, though, he's a questioner, never shuts up."

"Only because you never shut up, old man," Antony retorted lightheartedly while giving his companions an apologetic look. "Go on, Angus," he then encouraged with a wink. "Nothing else keeps him occupied like an entertaining story."

Angus faltered, unsure of what to say at first. Once the faucet of his mouth was turned on, however, the pure words flowed easily. "My brother and I spent a lot of our time over the summer at a resort my father owned. It was fun for us and easier for our parents. The staff of the water park and the hotel all knew us, and kept an eye out for us, like thousands of babysitters. My father would run his business and my mom would relax, because the help did all the cleaning and cooking for her. I think I was about seven when my brother convinced me to explore the underground network that the staff used to get from place to place. He had found it a day or two before; the hotel workers who occasionally ran errands to the park or beach frequented this door in the basement.

"I remember it was a hot day and we were going to spend it inside anyway, so I figured underground would be nice and cool while still fun—seven-year-old logic. We snuck in, took a few turns. It was pretty cold in there, as if the air-conditioning filtered its way through the cement halls. We bumped into a few workers, and, I don't quite remember how, but Giles—my brother—smooth talked them into leaving us alone. He must have bribed them or scared them, because they really did obey him. Maybe it's just because he knows how to act like my father. But anyway, we found one entrance and surprisingly, we were in the back room of a restaurant by the boardwalk. My mind at the time couldn't figure out how the hallways worked. I'd close the door to the restaurant and open it again, expecting a different result and finding no change. It was like taking a different route to the same, mundane destination. It gave me a brand new feeling, like I was rediscovering the resort I knew like the back of my hand.

"So, anyway, Giles probably got bored of it, or maybe he walked too quickly or I walked too quickly, but we lost each other in the tunnels. I started to cry, noisily; my voice seemed to ricochet off the walls. Time passed, and next thing I knew, evening had arrived and I was starving and utterly lost. Someone should have marked the walls with arrows or landmarks or something. Even now I can't imagine how the workers found their way around—or maybe that's just the way I remember it. Anyway, it turns out I was near the hotel, because my father, surprised, found me sniffling. Together, we searched the tunnels, which were somehow easy for him to navigate, for Giles. My bedtime back then was eight thirty, and I got sleepy. My father decided to bring me back to the hotel to put me to bed and to search more thoroughly for Giles afterwards. He made me promise not to tell my mother that Giles was missing—the rule was that we were allowed to venture out into the resort so long as we stuck together. Had my mother discovered we broke the rule, she would have freaked out, called the cops, something. I heard they found him soon enough, not underground, but on the surface, bothering the folks at ice cream stands for his favorite chocolate soft serve. I remember being half-awake as my father tucked Giles into bed. We didn't get yelled at and we all kept it a secret from my mom to this day. It's crazy now that … yeah."

Angus stopped, just a hint of a smile remaining on his face. He couldn't quite recall when everything began to change, but sure as the water licks the shore, everything did. His father grew into a hard and often disappointed-looking man, concerned only with business-y parts of life. He spent a lot of time on his laptop or phone, as if nothing else were more important than the next message or notification he'd receive. Often, Angus wondered how his soulful mother could have married such a tough-skinned man.

"Great story, kid," Sans said, meaning it. "You should bring your brother sometime. Reminisce together. I think it would do you two some good."

Angus half expected to snap at him for implying family troubles, but he didn't. "I think it would, too," he mumbled, looking thoughtful.

"What, is it our turn now?" Antony, who hadn't spoken extensively, gestured at himself and quiet Jessie. "I'm not going on a tirade about my entire life to you guys. Sans would have a heart attack at all the shit I've done."

"You've got nothing to back up that bark of yours," Angus accused.

"Oh yeah? I've got oak for bones, I'll have you know." An argument ensued in which Sans backed Angus, who tripped over computer wires walking across the room in agitation, and Antony kept his rear end planted on the beanie bag, laughing his comebacks away. "I don't want to get into this with you, man," he said coolly. "I'd kill you. It's real simple. I'd kill you and your fucking parents would sue me and it'd be a big mess and I don't care enough about you to bother."

Sans's attitude changed to one of concern at the threat. "Antony, you're not serious, are you? I could arrest you for that, you know."

"It's from the fucking *Breakfast Club*, chill out, man. Besides, I wouldn't hurt Angus—he's a little sweetheart." Antony lovingly banged his chest with his fist as if to demonstrate how his heart beat for him. "Right, Gus?"

Angus snapped, like an unrehearsed explosion, hissed from the corners of his mouth, "Don't you dare call me that."

"Ouch. Okay. I know of no other endearing nicknames for 'Angus.' Maybe I should just call you Beef. You're not particularly beefy, but—"

"Stop pissing out of your mouth," Sans said, finally sick of the banter. He returned his attention to the screens, examining them for movement. On floor E, a young woman exited her room and adjusted her coat before leaving toward the stairs.

Jessie peered at the screens. "She lives on our floor. Who is that? I've never seen her around."

Sans answered but didn't take his eyes off the screens. "That's Roonie. She's a fine young lady. Much like you, much like you." Roonie moved down the stairs, jumping from screen to screen.

"Hey," Antony piped in, "is it true that she's a—"

Sans swiveled in his chair rapidly and violently threw a stress ball toward him. His aim was perfect, as it whistled past Antony's ear and bounced off the wall behind him. The security guard said no more. Antony picked up the stress ball, examined it, and then said, "Yeah, sorry, that was dumb of me."

Jessie and Angus looked at each other, both wondering what, exactly, this Roonie character was, and why gentle Sans silently scolded Antony. The latter spoke up, voice sadly cheerful: "I have some stuff to do; you guys can go upstairs now."

"You sure?" Antony asked.

"Mhm, mhm."

Though plagued with locusts eating at their minds, they departed, restless, with nothing else to do but rest.

June brought July, only the month bore no flowers. The cityscape, painted in gray, saddened Jessie. She loved seeing the bright colors bounce off buildings and the trees bloom in the park, but summer was a faraway prospect not under her control. Due to the weather, which threatened to snow and lingered below freezing, Jessie's mother drove her to therapy that weekend.

Minutes into the session, Jessie and Hilde agreed to let her mother, Marie, join for today. It was pure convenience on her parent's part, and pure untimeliness on Jessie's, for she had relapsed just the day before, in a fit of ennui and addiction. As she shrugged off her hoodie and revealed her punctured skin, Marie sighed. "Oh, baby," she said, "why did you do that?" Jessie hated the reaction, although logically, she knew it was understandable. She felt scolded, as if she'd been playing on the train tracks instead of cutting herself twenty-some times.

Struggling to explain herself, she finally said that she didn't know. "I was bored and numb, and I guess I just wanted to feel something, you know?" Marie, of course, didn't know.

Hilde graciously explained what they'd discussed before Marie's entrance. There existed a summer trend in Jessie's biorhythm, a seasonal-affected disorder that worked backward from the usual. She found that she was sadder during the spring and summer months, and relapsed more often, so much so that she'd been placed in a hospital and a program the past two years. "It would be advisable to place her in a therapeutic program earlier in the summer," Hilde suggested, "to circumvent her going to the hospital." Marie nodded, chewing seriously on the therapist's words. "Jessie cannot be watched at all hours of the day. We must trust her to be okay at certain hours of the day, and we must admit her to a program to get the extra therapy she needs."

"My husband and I will think about it," Marie said, in her nervous, half-broken English.

Jessie inserted her input, "I don't want to go into a program. I'll be okay, I swear."

"We know you will try, Jessie, but relapses cannot be avoided," said Hilde. "I think your parents would rather be safe than sorry." They discussed other things, such as possibly increasing her medication with her psychiatrist and alternative, positive methods of coping, most of which Jessie was resistant to. She despised the very phrase "coping skills" and refused to believe that she ever had a problem "coping." It was she who decided to cut that first time, a miniscule puncture through a hand-drawn butterfly that failed to convince her otherwise. It was her decision, often spurred on by a consensus within her psyche, not a blind impulse.

Though, she had to admit, her relapse was the product of a frightening blind impulse. It meant that she was not ready yet, not prepared for happiness. She hadn't

CHAPTER THREE

suffered enough to earn it, to be worth it. So, she must suffer again this cold summer.

They left therapy, Jessie picking the saddest acoustic song to play on her iPad complement her mood. Despite having made new friends, despite Angus's apparent obsession with her, she still felt lousy returning home alone every night. Even if people enjoyed her presence, loneliness somehow prevailed. It was the one-two punch of her nonsensical ailment: lonely no matter what, yet too afraid to depend on someone else.

Marie pulled up at the Complexes, parked, and the two descended from the minivan. Too tired to brave the stairs, they chose to hitch a ride on the creaky elevator. When its doors opened, a redhead with a mass of curls and a slim Indian man emerged, apparently discussing some movie they had watched. Upon seeing Jessie, however, the taller one stopped in his tracks and grinned at her, as if he was infinitely glad to see her. "Hey, Nathan, this is the girl Gus is hitting on."

"For real?" The Nathan character said, squinting at her.

Sensing Jessie's discontent at being examined, the Indian man added, "I apologize for being rude. I'm Giles Speare, Gus's brother. The half-wit staring at you is Nathan. We're a little late, so we should be going now, Miss and Mrs. Rivera." He inclined his head respectfully toward the two and took the other man's sleeve, plucking him away.

"You'd think that Angus would be a little peeved at the short hair."

"He's not that closed minded. Besides, she's pretty."

"Not that closed minded? He called me a fuckin' faggot a month ago."

Once Jessie, red-faced, entered the elevator, she hastily pressed the button to close the door and relieve herself of the awkward embarrassment of meeting Giles Speare and his companion. Angus hardly spoke of Giles, yet she somehow knew he was a character, a bit bizarre yet remarkably polite all the same. In comparison, Giles was taller and darker in skin, more angles than curves. He certainly was attractive, in that effortless way. She concluded that the entire Speare family carried the gene for chiseled good looks. Or perhaps it was the mixed blood.

Her iPad beeped. Probably Angus. When she checked—she was right, of course—he inquired as to what she was up to, if she was doing anything tonight. That message was oddly straightforward of Angus, who preferred to make plans far in advance over candidly asking. "No," she responded. "Just getting home from errands with my mom."

When the doors opened to reveal floor E, there stood Angus, pink in the cheeks from an unidentified emotion. "Oh,

CHAPTER THREE

Jessie," he exhaled, seemingly surprised, "and Mrs. Rivera." He fiddled absentmindedly with the messenger bag slung over his shoulder as he asked, anxiously, "Can I talk to you, Jessie?"

"Sure," she responded, looking at her mother. "Can he come over for dinner?"

Marie agreed, advising Angus that she only had Filipino food prepared tonight. Of course, he didn't mind, so long as he could have his allotted time with Jessie. "I'm sorry for barging in," he said as Marie unlocked the door to E02. "I actually wanted to catch Jessie as she was coming up the elevator—I didn't expect to be right." The two assured him that it was all right, that they liked having guests, that his presence wouldn't be a bother, just a delight. Angus, who was unfamiliar with Jessie's parents, was nervous anyway, for he was eager to please.

E02 was quaintly decorated with trinkets from family vacations, from Las Vegas to Manila. Each surface, though covered with pictures, souvenirs, or Catholic figures, was meaningfully covered, not cluttered. While Marie heated the food, Jessie presented her room to Angus; its tan walls and beige rug gave off a minimalist vibe, although it was a tad untidy with clothes and shoes. On the far wall, she had pinned up posters of famous artwork, book and movie posters, and store-bought canvases. "I didn't know you were into art,"

Angus remarked, ashamed that this topic hadn't previously been breached.

"I'm a dilettante, as they say," Jessie said, contorting her face at her own amateurish hobby. "I can't wait to go to college and take an art course, actually learn about all the paintings that I've seen." She ran her hand across a print of Matisse's *The Goldfish*, which actually also hung in Hilde's office. "It must be wonderful, being an artist."

Angus watched her, the way her eyes twinkled and her hands constantly moved when she got passionate. "You should meet my mom," he said, "She loves art, too. My parents got married in a chapel in Florence. In fact," he paused, studying her angled eyes and lightly tanned skin, "you remind me a lot of her. My mom, I mean. I hope that's not creepy."

A slow grin spread across Jessie's face. "That's the ultimate compliment a guy can give a girl, did you know that? Thank you."

While they ate the *sinigang* Marie prepared, the three of them made small talk about school and where they were going to go from there. "Right now my dad's the manager of this pharmacy," Angus explained, "so I was thinking of going into business like him."

At that, Jessie expressed her surprise, for she never pegged him as a business major. "I could never do something like that,"

CHAPTER THREE

she admitted. "I just want to read and look at art and watch movies."

"Maybe you should be a critic," he suggested. Marie approved wholeheartedly, and Jessie simply smiled into her dinner at the concept. Before, she hadn't thought of that. "You could tell people they suck if they suck and tell others that they're amazing, and they'd take it to heart because you'd be a professional at it. Sounds like a good deal to me."

After dinner, Angus followed Jessie into her room and sat on the bed. "So?" she asked, sitting cross-legged beside him. "What's the big to-do?"

"Huh?"

"What did you want to talk to me about?"

"Right," Angus said, fidgeting, wearing an agitated expression. "I don't think it's that important anymore." He looked at her almost pleadingly, like a child needing to be excused to the bathroom. Jessie, half-tempted to pursue the topic, relented; he sighed in what sounded like relief. "I'm sorry for wasting your time," he apologized, which didn't occur unless he was infringing upon someone's hospitality.

Jessie forgave him, despite her desperate curiosity. Everyone wanted to know the happenings in the war fought on home ground in E01. While Angus battled for intimacy with Jessie, he simultaneously neglected a most pivotal issue that could, with proper discussion, result in that intimacy. Jessie simply couldn't understand why he remained so distant—but then, reminded of the cuts on her arm, all of which remained unknown to Angus, she changed her mind. She could, indeed, understand.

Friendship and romance were too much of a game, and nowadays Jessie often hadn't had the heart to play it. Her few friends in school were simply that—girls to sit next to during the school hours. Antony, perhaps, seemed like someone who would take her revelations either well or badly. Angus? The same story as Antony, only more extreme due to his heightened care for her. And she still couldn't fathom why he cared so much for a girl he knew essentially so little about.

Yet, she was growing to care for him. He no longer was a nuisance to text, but a rock she could, hypothetically, learn to depend on should she urgently need it. He also kept her life rather interesting, what with his untrained mouthiness when around Antony and his secret home life. Perhaps it was the prolonged communication that eventually tied them together, made them feel closer then they truly were.

As if sensing what Jessie was thinking, Angus offered, "If I were to kiss you right now, and it would mean absolutely nothing but a kiss, would you be okay with that?"

CHAPTER THREE

She looked at him, at first unsure. Then her eyes flickered to his lips, slightly parted, breathing. Goddamnit, she wasn't supposed to give in like this. She wasn't ready, remember? Not ready for a relationship again, not ready to throw her delicate life in someone else's just as delicate hands.

When she kissed him, he grasped her left arm to pull her closer. Her fresh wounds stung, but it was, in that moment, okay.

COMPLEXES

Chapter Four

The last time Antony resided in the Complexes, it was for a brief four months celebrating Ruthy's quiet marriage to Thomas, a robust man who served as her dramatic foil. While she smoked everywhere but around her seven-year-old, he refused addictive substances of any kind to maintain his health. She was coarse and reluctantly motherly; he was more than glad and willing to increase the family's numbers by one, even if Morrissey's parentage was questionable. Even now, Ruthy refuses to acknowledge Morrissey's father's existence. Even Gerard did not know, but he always said he could make an educated guess based on the girl's chubbier cheeks and stubborn freckles.

But Antony, twelve years old at the time, had no concern for the familial drama. As far as he was concerned, Morrissey was Thomas's child—she clung onto him like a cat on a scratch post. He, a good man and father, always provided childish tokens like milkshakes and sweets behind Ruthy's strict back, and told her that he loved her quite often, often enough that it stuck in her Teflon mind.

How Ruthy and Thomas, two opposites, met, Antony didn't know. Ruthy claimed modestly to have met him through chains of friends; Thomas joked they met on

CHAPTER FOUR

a cruise across the Mediterranean. Nevertheless, Gerard, the only other family member present and the man who gave Ruthy away at the ceremony, seemed to approve wholeheartedly of the relationship, saying it was a "healthy alternative" to her previous relationships. But Antony's one rule living in the Complexes back then was not to mess with Ruthy, who rasped a rage and coldheartedly served dinner, so he never asked about those unhealthy relationships.

Now that Antony was older, however, such rules were thrown out of the window, far into the harbor. He, all too curious to discover what happened to the tender Thomas, often asked his father only to receive a shrug in return. It was only a matter of time until he directed his investigation towards Morrissey, who, surprisingly, seemed not at all affected by the divorce. In fact, Ruthy did not look all too bothered, either. This led Antony to conclude that the separation was a calm, mutual event—or a cold, numbing decision.

The latter was more interesting, and Antony was inclined to pursue the interesting.

"What do you think?" he deliberated with his father. "Should I ask Morrissey?"

"I think you're being too nosy; you might hurt the little girl," Gerard wisely suggested.

Ultimately, his advice went unheeded. Antony breached the topic one Sunday while helping clean E06, vacuuming, doing laundry, and such. Once Ruthy exited to buy groceries, he shut off the suctioning machine and said rather bluntly in the ensuing silence, "What happened to Thomas?"

Morrissey was curled up on a couch, doing everything in her power not to help Antony clean, while reading a book covered in her annotations. "He left," she said, pausing before casually turning the page.

"Yeah, I guessed that much," Antony doggedly continued, leaning on the vacuum haphazardly. "But I mean, what happened?"

With an exasperated sigh, as if she were working with preschoolers, she closed her book and stood up. "How do I put it lightly?" she deliberated. "It's none of your fucking business. Now if you'll excuse me, your presence is killing my brain cells." She exited grandly, leaving only dark markings on the carpet where she'd stood.

It so bothered him that he even brought it up with Jessie and Angus, who both explicitly avoided discussing personal affairs even when he more than happily rubbed his business in their faces. "It's the reason I'm in this depressing city in the first place," he complained. "I might as well figure out what the hell happened, right?" No response, because both thought, like everyone else, that Antony was simply too meddlesome for his own good. "Right," he answered himself.

CHAPTER FOUR

"What happened with you and your husband?" Antony inquired as politely as he could manage, as Ruthy clipped coupons from magazines. After giving him a dangerous look over her glasses, she sliced a coupon out—*snip!*—and placed it in her orderly pile. The subject, consequently, was not pursued.

When all else failed, he approached Sans, who listened to his desperation whilst absentmindedly braiding strands of his beard. "You've been here awhile. Give me a clue, something, anything," Antony pleaded.

Like everyone else, Sans refused to help. Unlike everyone else, he occasionally burped information and excused himself rather belatedly. Antony's eyes brightened at the newfound information, and he rushed out of the security office, nearly bumped into an angry Miriam ("No one is allowed in there!"), and climbed the stairs like a frenzied gorilla. "A piece of the puzzle has been acquired!" he announced upon his entrance to E11, disrupting his father's habitual daydreaming.

Needless to say, when he presented his evidence and theory to Ruthy, she was not pleased. "I'm disappointed, Antony."

"What? Am I wrong?"

"No, you are not wrong." Taking off her glasses, she wiped them with the hem of her shirt, revealing the kind of blue eyes that saw and felt things. "I'm just disappointed."

COMPLEXES

Ruthy had cheated on Thomas with Morrissey's real father. She had openly confessed to her mistake, but forgiveness was too expensive a cost. Thomas left the next morning, bequeathing a great sum of money dedicated to Morrissey's education. "She's a smart girl," he told Ruthy over coffee, hand resting on the handle of his packed suitcase. "She deserves the world."

Out of fear that she would choose Thomas over Ruthy, they mutually decided to leave her in the dark. Morrissey would never learn the truth.

After the failed coffee truce of June, Jonathan ceased to believe that he owed anything to the Speare family, be it an explanation or consolation. Still, he felt contrite toward Mara, the mother, whom Giles resembled strikingly. Especially after overhearing James's morning conversation with Giles, he felt as though she were being punished for her husband's mistakes. Screw Angus and James—if he could apologize to her, his guilty conscious would be more at ease.

On some days more than often he thought of her and of his own mother, distant and conservative in her views. His sophomore year of college he moved out of his asphyxiating household and set up shop with a boyfriend in the Complexes, in the cheaper area of the city. Thus a new era of Jonathan's life began, freed from expectations and his father's homophobic remarks and slaps. Instead of pursuing biology, which he initially applied for, he took up the paintbrush, often painting in heavy chiaroscuro and the intimate tenebrism of the Baroque. Simultaneously he yearned to become an artist in his own right, to discover his own style and join a modern movement.

Something held him back. He had plenty of connections and strange bedfellows to consult with, and his professors praised his ability to depict his figures in a multitude of styles. However, he wasn't excellent, often receiving lower grades for his lack of originality. "Find yourself," advised a professor during Jonathan's early career, looking at him carefully behind thick glasses.

"Haven't I found myself already?" questioned he who was finally liberated from the mothballs in the closet. It seemed his journey of self-discovery would never end, and, to be quite frank, he was growing tired of overthinking and analyzing himself. If he could live off his cheap imitations of Caravaggio, he figured he'd still be satisfied. Perhaps success wasn't what he ultimately yearned for.

Nowadays, his mind was occupied with one person.

COMPLEXES

"Tea at Martha's?" Giles suggested after many movies, rubbing his eyes and then warming his left hand with his right. Jonathan agreed wholeheartedly, because he enjoyed the presence of the hunchbacked old woman and he enjoyed how she treated them like a legitimate couple. Together, they traipsed to E10 and politely entreated to enter, waiting at least five minutes for her to shuffle to the door and open it for them.

The silver-haired elder's wrinkle of a smile spread at the sight of the boys. "Oh, dear, you young men flatter me." She giggled about as they gathered around the small table designated expressly for afternoon tea. "Always keeping little old me company, how sweet of you."

"Let me get that," Giles said, referring to the hissing kettle. Martha hummed her consent as Jonathan plucked certain flavors of loose tea, today deciding on black Darjeeling, packed little tea bags, and placed them in dainty teacups. Giles's slim hands poured the boiling water over the bags, and the aroma filled the room like the rising swirls of steam. Giles liked his tea without sugar or milk; the other two immediately began adding condiments to their preference. They waited a minute or two, and sipped in silence.

Halfway through his cup, Jonathan asked, "How have you been, Mrs. Schmidt?" After all these months, he hadn't the guts to abandon formalities and call her Martha.

CHAPTER FOUR

On the other hand, Giles was perfectly content being on a first-name basis with a woman more than triple his age.

Her voice always shook slightly, as if she were singing her vowels with vibrato. "Oh, I've been just dandy, Mr. Gillian. Although I'm afraid my arthritis has me calling the pharmacy more than I'd like. I wish they'd just give me more Advil ..." The woman was strangely addicted to over-the-counter painkillers, so much so that the pharmacy refused to fuel her dependence by delivering more than necessary to her.

Consoling her as best as they could, Giles teased that his back and neck always ached and Jonathan pretended to suffer from carpal tunnel. "I'm getting *old*," whined the latter, massaging his hands with a hint of a grin on his Cheshire face.

Giles corroborated, "Some people age nicely like you, Martha. I hope when I gray I gray like a mad scientist." It was a lie; Martha had hardly aged nicely. All of her problems would have rendered her an invalid were it not for muscle rubs and medications. She suffered from hair loss, leaving tufts of pearly-white hair on her pillow every morning. But she believed the boys' banter all the same, mostly because she considered them handsome copies of her boyfriends in her youth.

"You need a haircut desperately, Mr. Gillian," commented Martha, reaching her hand over to his mane of curls. "I used to cut my own hair, you know," she said, and, convinced that she still had the ability to snip and trim Jonathan's, began rummaging around drawers for scissors.

Smiling yet terrified, he stopped her and guided her back to her chair. "It's okay," he reassured her, "I'll get it cut before I see you next, I promise."

While on their second cup and round of biscuits, Martha inquired what the boys were up to. They described as colorfully as possible the movies they've watched—all strange in their own right, independent and unconventional. "The effects to this one were horrible," Jonathan explained. "But the concept was interesting. People fought with words—like if you said 'fire,' fire would appear and engulf your enemy." He leaned forward, eyes aimed at his companion, "An inferno swallows you and gnaws your skin down to your bones."

Accepting the challenge, Giles coolly replied with effective brevity, "Waters kiss away the licking flames."

With only a second to think, Jonathan hastily continued, "A spill of oil mucks your ocean, slows and suffocates the fish."

"Burn the oil like a scab off the surface," came the quick, almost thoughtless comeback. "The resulting toxics slide into your mouth like a tongue." Jonathan's face twitched, his pale freckles burned a bright red at the simile. Goddamnit, why did he have to seduce him so aggressively? "I win," Giles confirmed, taking a celebratory sip of his tea. Jonathan couldn't argue, for he had hesitated far too long. Pouting, he crossed his arms and legs and looked away until his blush faded.

"What happened?" Martha asked, the conversation flying entirely over her head. Giles's hearty laugh only embarrassed Jonathan further.

Teacups emptied and delicately washed, they said their good-byes to twittering old Martha and exited E10. They walked down the hallway back to E07. Before Jonathan took out his keys to unlock the door, he hesitated, and asked, hiding his agitation, "Why all the kissing references, Giles? Are you eager to head out on a Friday night escapade or are you implying something?"

With a trained blank face, he responded neutrally, "Would you like me to be implying something?"

As usual, Jonathan hadn't a clue whether he was being flirtatious or platonic. He turned, back against the door, and his eyes purposefully flitted to Giles's lips and back up to his eyes, as if presenting both a response and a challenge. A minute elapsed, the two simply standing there, staring the other down. "Take the bait, for godssake," Jonathan almost pleaded. "I love you, goddamnit. I love how smart you are and how you watch movies, cross-legged and leaning forward and mouth slightly ajar, as if you were mouthing every word. I love how controlling and yet how reluctant you are, like right now, damn it." He ran a hand through his hair in a "forget-it" kind of motion, slapped his cheeks, and pulled the loudly jingling keys from his pocket.

That night, rather than watch more movies, they went out to a club and separated, Jonathan searching for another tall Indian man to play pretend with. Empty-handed, he watched Giles in the arms of another man, as tall and stout as an athlete, laughing and rotating on the dance floor. He figured, maybe with enough drinks he could pry his love away and lovingly punish him behind closed hotel room doors. Even with another shot, he didn't have the heart.

The next morning, Giles told him that he was meeting this man again. "It doesn't usually happen," he said, "but I almost like him." That was enough for him.

I wash my hands of this, decided Jonathan, thinking of Mara, trying not to think of Giles. From that point on, Giles had matured beyond Jonathan's wing.

"I don't like any of them," protested Angus, feeling like a child but unable to help himself. His mother exasperatedly sighed, flipped her lengthy hair to the other side of her shoulder, and examined the rows and rows of eyeglasses her son had to choose from. Angus had struggled with reading the board in school for years, had basically failed the unfailable eye exam, and yet he refused the curse of glasses. "I'll look stupid," was his excuse. But once Mara told him that he couldn't begin driving due to his impaired vision, he relented.

The young woman working as the doctor's assistant was carefully patient with Angus, as if she had endured many kids, albeit years younger than Angus, who similarly despised the concept of four eyes. "Try this, it's very stylish." She offered a large pair of aviator glasses. Angus rudely grimaced at the sight of them and stormed out of the store, leaving his embarrassed mother to clean up the social mess he left behind.

He didn't know why he always had to be so damn hardheaded. His face burned from the humiliation. Angus was always careful about his appearance, as he had admitted to himself since his youth that Giles's easy handsomeness rendered him jealous. His slim build threatened to become unwieldy, like his father's, and his face still resembled a baby's. Everything about his facial features looked big—his nose, his lips, his cheeks, his eyes; when he focused on any one of them, it blew up like a balloon in his imagination. He didn't know what glasses would do to him. He was, in short, stubborn, afraid of change, and too insecure to admit it.

Mara had excused herself and joined her son outside, leaning against the wall

134

with him. "We can leave," she said, squinting out into the breeze.

"And not learn how to drive?" he scoffed. "I'm not giving up that luxury."

His mother breathed deeply before saying, "You're not making sense, Angus. What do you want? What do you really want?"

There were plenty of things that he could want. He wanted a smartphone, the ability to drive, a refill on his subway card. He wanted to listen to a song his father used to like and not think of his father. He wanted to be able to tell his mother everything and yet tell her nothing. He wanted Jessie. He wanted his old brother back, the one that didn't drink and wasn't gay and wrapped his arms around his parents to bring them closer in family pictures.

"I'll get the glasses," he murmured, returning to the office and choosing the large black square ones, the ones that settled snugly on his nose and made his eyes look proportionate to the remainder of his face. Mara called him handsome, and he was inclined to believe her.

They left the eye doctor's and boarded a subway, homebound. As they disembarked, a voice called from behind, "Mara!" The formless voice startled the two of them, who both looked to multiple directions for its owner. "Mara," it repeated, closer this time. "It's me, Gerard." An adequately tall blond man in a suit waved at them, approaching. Angus was not on a first-name basis with him, but he recalled seeing him a few times in Antony's apartment—he was Antony's father.

"Oh, what a coincidence," Mara exclaimed. "Are you heading somewhere special?"

"Home from work, if you can call that special," he replied, scratching his forehead, "And you and your son ... Angus, if I remember correctly?"

Angus had to admit, he was impressed with the man's ability to maintain the connection between names and faces. His mother smiled at him brightly, with a polite verve that she hardly wore at home anymore. "Heading home from an appointment," she explicated, adjusting the bag on her shoulder.

"Then I suppose we're heading in the same direction. Shall we?" Gerard allowed Mara to begin walking first and followed after Angus, though remaining close. "How was the dinner you had? That miso salmon?"

She remarked, "What a memory of yours! I hardly remember yesterday's dinner."

"If it's not especially prominent in your mind, it was probably okay. Gosh, I miss my mother's cooking. You've got it made, kid." Angus only realized he was being spoken to when the conversation lulled obviously; he filled the void by supplying a blunt affirmative. Already, his

136

opinion of Gerard began forming in his mind. He was amiable, perhaps too much so, to the point of prying, just like his son. In fact, Angus pegged him as a significantly more mature Antony, whose overtalkative habits are slowly dying a hard death.

Mara chuckled. "I'm really not that great. My mother's cooking, however, *that* was great." Angus perked up at the mention of his mother's previous life in India, which was normally seldom discussed. Perhaps she had brought it up simply for conversation's sake? Was he overthinking things, as usual, or …?

"Oh really? Probably can't beat my mother's meat loaf," teased Gerard.

"Curry and meat loaf are two entirely different things," she replied with equal energy.

Were they flirting? Unabashedly flirting right in front of him? They now walked side by side, as if deliberately cutting Angus out of the line of conversation. He watched how she beamed at him, teeth peeking out, her olive skin practically glowing. Angus grew visibly red at the very sight of it.

Along their walk, they touched on many subjects, from their mothers to their childhoods to what they were having for dinner tonight. "I never learned how to properly cook," Gerard admitted sheepishly, "so we go for frozen dinners and microwavables a lot."

CHAPTER FOUR

They entered the Complexes and, from Mara's lead, decided to take the elevator. "I'm surprised all the preservatives haven't stunted your son's growth. If you ever need a proper dinner, you're always welcome. I always cook more than planned, so it wouldn't be a problem."

The doors slid open and they stepped into the roomy yet undecorated enclosed space while Gerard accepted the offer without taking her up on it. "I really couldn't intrude," he maintained rather coyly.

"Oh please. Don't be shy. I bet your son misses his mother's cooking, too."

This sobered Gerard up considerably. "Yes," he chose to say, "I bet he does." Mara noticed that she had touched on a taboo topic; she promptly sewed her mouth shut in embarrassment. The elevator dinged appropriately, letting on no one but a pink, fat, elephant. Silence ensued.

"I'm sorry," she said apprehensively once they reached floor E. "I said something wrong."

"Antony never knew his mother," he told her, with such quiet intimacy that Angus had almost forgotten that he, himself, was intruding on this moment. "She left when he was very young."

Mara's eyebrows knit closer together, and her eyes expressed genuine sympathy. "I'm so sorry," she echoed herself. In a lighter tone, she added, "All the more reason to come and visit. I mean it, okay?"

138

COMPLEXES

Gerard flashed a smile. "Okay." With clear hesitation, he walked his short distance, said his good-byes, and disappeared into E11.

Angus glanced at his mother, trying to discern her current state of mind. Mara appeared troubled yet simultaneously serene, like a wave licking the shore. Noticing her son's inquisitive look, she grinned briefly and began her advance into the suffocating E01. Once they entered and she shrugged off her coat, Angus bombarded her with his boiling questions. "What was all that about? All that smiling and giggling?"

Mara sighed a half sigh and half groan—run as she might, she couldn't catch a break. "I was just making polite conversation."

"Maybe a tad too polite," he persisted.

Snapping, she gripped the hem of her coat. "So you get to police how I talk now?"

"I don't like the way he looked at you and how you so gladly reciprocated," Angus stated. He'd well thought it out during the ride on the elevator.

"Yes, the way he looked at me was polite," she argued, using her hands demonstratively, waving the coat around. "So I was polite in return."

He swallowed, feeling the heat run through his nose and up to his eyes. "All I'm saying is, if I don't get to leave this hellhole, you sure as hell aren't allowed to, either."

CHAPTER FOUR

His knees buckled, allowing him to collapse onto the couch, framing his contorted face with his hand. "There," he concluded, "I said it."

Mara understood. After hanging up her previously flailing coat, she approached her son with compassion written palpably on her face. Gingerly she placed her hand on his back, moving it in circles like she would to soothe a hiccupping baby. Not a word escaped from her, even if she had a thousand things to say to him.

Finally, Angus asked the hanging question: "Do you ever look at Father that way?"

She stared blankly down at the floor, decorated with arabesque rugs, avoiding the blank stares of wedding photographs set in the world's most beautiful city. "Once upon a time," she said.

And Angus knew that things were going to fall apart, that they were bound to. Perhaps, a thought flitted through his mind like the devil on his red wings, his older brother was right in escaping when he did.

Neither Angus nor Antony bothered to explore the vast city at their disposal, so Jessie felt it was her obligation to reveal to them her favorite spots to visit. Only a few weeks had passed since their friendship first bloomed, but, as circumstance would have it, the three had become weirdly close, like tissues that just happened to be in the same packaging. They practiced a tacit habit of waiting for each other in the subway station before going home together discussing the happenings of the Complexes. Aside from that, they hardly saw each other—a fact that Jessie wished to change.

Jessie had trouble in social situations. Her anxiety trumped her yearning to make friends, and the friends she had she held at a respectable distance. Her fear of infringing upon healthy boundaries prevented her from disclosing personal information, such as what she did every weekend and why she got unbearably cranky during the period between her menstruation and ovulation. School friends were just that, people to sit with during class and lunch. Angus and Antony, however, were more than that. She could easily dismiss them as neighborly friends, but after Antony guessed gleefully that she and Angus had, indeed, kissed, she somehow knew she could not push everyone away.

So she organized a Friday night, just the three of them, during which they would venture into the city full of prospects and life. "We're going to this awesome place that still sells Polaroids. And—oh, nearby is a flea market, a Japanese novelty shop, and a place that sells pizza in cones ..." Rare excitement bubbled up in her as she scrolled around the map of the city on her phone, identifying streets of interest.

CHAPTER FOUR

Antony and Angus nodded, accepted her enthusiasm with openness.

They entered the film store via an elevator whose speed rivaled the one in the Complexes. Each dished out two dollars to pay for a Polaroid portrait, taken in a photo booth just like the ones at the entrances of movie theatres. They exchanged the resulting pictures, so each had a one of the other. Jessie sighed wistfully as she marveled at the reconstructions of cameras lined up on minimalistic white shelves. Antony, meanwhile, wondered whether or not his father kept photos of his mother around. If so, he had never glimpsed them.

"I've never tried this before," Jessie admitted when they entered the pizza place, which was covered in alternating red and white tiles with a modern vibe. They ordered, sat down. Angus excused himself shortly into the meal, stomping outside with his pizza cone in tow. When he returned he was wiping his mouth with the back of his hand; he was a picky eater, and something about the pizza rubbed his taste buds the wrong way. From then on, traditionalist Angus was permanently opposed to the concept of pizza in cones.

They mingled with an eclectic blend of people at the flea market, whose vendors sold vintage clothes and antique goods at what they called a "reasonable price." More there to browse than to shop, Jessie admired the one-of-a-kind earrings to match with her cropped hair; Angus, who was impressed by

COMPLEXES

Jessie's poster collection, searched through old advertisements, and Antony conversed casually with whichever seller caught his attention. "It's so easy for you to talk," she said with envy. He shrugged and claimed it was an inborn skill.

Angus and Antony felt sorely out of place in the novelty store full of pastels, lace, trinkets, and Hello Kitty toys and stationery. Jessie went to town with all the cute baubles while the boys stood back and allowed her to have her fun.

It was there that Angus dropped the bomb he'd been holding in his chest. The mood between the two changed so strikingly that when Jessie returned, having purchased some colored pens for her organized note taking, she immediately noticed the shift. She hesitated to ask if something was wrong, as she instantly convinced herself that she was responsible for it. Were they bored? Did they not like the little Japanese bookstore? Had she committed a sin of commission, or of omission?

The boys remained pointedly civil toward each other, but whatever friendliness they once shared had gone. Jessie found herself straining to keep the conversation at a favorable tide as it often teetered toward awkward silence. As she spoke, she hoped they didn't hear how out-of-body it was, how fake her cheerfulness was. The day had commenced on a wonderful, yet concise, note. Jessie noticed one solid fact about her days: there was always a catch, a reason to go to sleep upset.

They parted ways at the Complexes, on floor E. Because E11 was the closest to the elevator, Antony was the first to vacate the hallway. "See ya," he said, saluting them nonchalantly, clearly relieved to be dismissed.

"Bye, Angus," Jessie said, reaching her doorknob reluctantly. "Thanks for the day."

"Wait." He stopped her, shoved his hands in his pockets, and looked down at the ground. "Never mind. Have a good night."

She closed and then leaned on the door, exhausted from the day's more mentally stressful events. Never before had she felt so connected to people—not since her ex-boyfriend whom she never liked to think about and never wanted to repeat. Remaining distant hurt her, but now that she wanted friends they always seemed to fall apart at the seams when she stretched them just a little. In her room, on loose leaf paper, she wrote a thousand times with her new, clear black pen bought in that little Japanese novelty store, *It logically cannot be my fault.* Logically it was true, but emotionally?

Jessie couldn't handle friends. She was beginning to think she didn't deserve them.

COMPLEXES

She wouldn't know for a long time that Angus had asked Antony to tell his father to back off his mother, just as she wouldn't know that Antony had refused to police his father on the sole word of a paranoid son. She wouldn't know for a long time that it truly had nothing to do with her. She wouldn't know, and that would eventually help her ruin.

Roonie didn't dislike her job; she disliked her coworker, boss, or subordinate, whatever the night called it. It had gotten to the point when she could identify what kind of person she'd be working with by what kind of hotel room they'd book. The fancier the room, the more rough they would be. If the hotel was grimy, usually the bookers were first-timers who simply desired some love. Of course, there were exceptions to the rule.

Even though she had handled Giles in an apartment, he was one of those exceptions. He didn't seek love or a good time—in fact, she hardly knew what he wanted. Beginning harsh and ending gentle, he looked right through her, into something else. She recognized that look in many young lovers, but she didn't peg him as an archetype. Jonathan clearly wasn't joking when he said she had a big job with Giles.

"Instead of squandering all your money, why don't you deal with him yourself?" she asked Jonathan, who stood at her doorway, eyes pleading. He refused, mumbling something about Giles being a brother to him. So she agreed, because she did owe Jonathan a favor for bailing her out of a sticky situation.

Someone had given the police a tip that she was a prostitute. Perhaps that one video of her leaked online and a local porn digger recognized her from it? Nevertheless, when she saw the black-and-white car park itself outside of her window, she knew they were coming for her.

Jonathan was fairly new to the Complexes at that point. He respected the tacit rule that no one reports the obvious prostitute next door, and he even extended that respect directly to her in their brief passing conversations in the hallway. Vaguely, she remembered him mention that he was an art student living off-campus to get the whole "city experience." Using that fact to her advantage, she rushed to his door and hastily entreated him to set up shop in her apartment, easel, oils, and all. Jonathan sensed her urgency and complied without an opposing word.

When the police rapped on the door of E08, Jonathan answered, paintbrush and pen lodged between his teeth. "What?" he struggled to enunciate in a nonchalant matter. Spitting out his utensils, he said, "Is there something wrong, Officer?"

Miriam, who hovered behind the man, swooned at the sight of Roonie, lying obliquely on the couch, naked save well-placed girly Japanese stickers on her dark nipples. On Jonathan's easel was a hurried preliminary sketch of his subject. The officer's expression also betrayed his awkwardness, but he remained professionally calm as he presented his warrant.

"Can it wait?" Jonathan asked, anxious to continue sketching. "I'm a bit inspired."

Of course, an artist's inspiration was second to the law. Jonathan was sidestepped, and the officer examined the apartment, opening drawers and displacing clothes. Roonie looked appropriately apprehensive and asked what was wrong. "We've received a tip about you," explained the cop, "that you've been self-prostituting." With his gloved hands, he plucked up piles of lingerie from a particular drawer. Roonie bit her lip.

"I can assure you that she isn't," said Jonathan defensively. "She visits a lot of art students and artists, like me, as a nude model." He gestured toward his own imaginative interpretation of the womanly form. "Didn't you say something about your ex-boyfriend, Ronald?"

She looked to her accomplice, eyes wide in confusion. Sure, she had plenty of ex-boyfriends, but none named Ronald. Jonathan nodded confidently in her direction. Improvising, she said, "Oh, Ronald. He's a jealous one. Are you sure the tip didn't come from him? He was very … overzealous when we broke up recently."

Looking underneath Roonie's bed, the officer discovered three shoeboxes filled to the brim with cash. The fourth was a quarter empty. Roonie quickly supplied, "I don't trust the bank."

Despite all the effort, Roonie was taken in for questioning, and thereon she refused to say anything without her lawyer present. When she was released a short time later due to a lack of evidence—having a loose sex life was not against the law—she joked to Jonathan that she lied her whole way through it, and was entirely too pleased with herself. "No less thanks to you," she said to him over drinks the next week, a month before he would meet Giles.

Nowadays, the two were considered one in her mind. They acted like a couple, living together and going everywhere, but were everything but. She almost felt invasive the days she watched movies with them, Jonathan splayed on the couch and Giles sitting cross-legged on a pillow on the ground. Yet, she envied their ability to banter and then fall into silence, embracing the pregnant elephant. Those two were meant to be, she figured, and the one night she came between that was uncomfortable as hell.

COMPLEXES

One day, Jonathan invited Roonie to a friendly dinner at the Chouette Chouette. With no work that night and a curious mind, she accepted, wondering why now, of all times, was the artist not travelling with his brush. When she sat down across from him at the diner, she immediately asked, "Where's Giles?"

Jonathan deflated visibly at the mention of his missing partner. "With this new guy, Mano."

She snorted. "Mano?"

"Nickname," he elucidated, rolling his eyes as well. "His name is Hugo Manning. But because of his blue fauxhawk, he goes by Mano, which is apparently Hawaiian for shark."

Roonie smirked, imagining an overly confident, tall white kid with endeavoring to copy *SLC Punk*. "I see what kind of a guy this Mano is already."

"Exactly my point!" Jonathan responded, enthusiastically gesticulating to express his frustration. "And Giles is all over him. He looks and acts so juvenile. I don't understand. I really don't get it." Hands trembling with caffeine, he offhandedly asked the waiter for another cup of his poison. "What's more, they're on an actual date tonight. Giles doesn't do dates. But apparently, he will for motherfucking Mano."

CHAPTER FOUR

Finally, she capitalized on her observations. "Am I hearing some jealousy on this line?"

"Not jealousy!" protested Jonathan. "I'm worried about Giles's mental state of mind!"

"Okay, okay, stop shouting," Roonie advised, pushing the coffee provided by the waiter to the far side of the table, away from him. "Don't give me that bullshit. My clients give me enough of that to wade around in for hours. You're in love and green with envy."

He groaned into his hands, slapped his cheeks twice motivationally, but didn't reach for his coffee. "Is it bad that I love him?"

Roonie could tell by his desperation, the half smile and half frown lingering on his mouth, that it was his first time admitting it out loud. "No," she answered, "it's not bad."

Jonathan then ranted for thirty minutes about his developing feelings for him. It was not love at first sight; no, it was lust. But denying himself that pleasure taught him how to respect Giles for his layered manner of speaking, for his heavy eyelashes, for his odd appreciation for strange things like mystery DVDs. He explained that he never made a move for fear of getting too entangled in his drama, in his destructive home life. The fact that he hadn't yet slept with or kissed or touched Giles was his only vindication from the homewrecking accusation. But now, while this squinty-eyed Mano character dated him, Jonathan felt robbed of something he never truly owned.

For the first time in her career, Roonie apologized for sleeping with someone. She felt that she owed Jonathan that much. "It should have been you that night," she said, "and I think Giles feels the same way."

However, he shied away from her encouraging words. "I think I need to let go. But thanks for listening."

"Anytime."

She parted ways with Jonathan at the door of the Chouette Chouette, deciding to retire early this evening. Chewing on the concept of love, Roonie had to wonder what had ruined her own love life—her job, or herself? What had ruined Jonathan's—his circumstances, or himself? It was a question she had never considered prior to this conversation, and it quickly became a major one that dogged her and barked at her and nipped at her heels.

When she reentered the Complexes, she was greeted by a grand, tattooed, bearded man whom she'd seen before but never quite noticed. "Can I talk to you in my office?" he boomed, not waiting for an answer before leading the way. Roonie reluctantly complied, hand in her bag, grasping the pepper spray she always carried around for protection. After leading her to the security office, floor covered in electric wires and the corner decorated like a teen hangout, he made his offer. "I know about your job. I'd like to meet you a month from now at the hotel on Lafayette and Church Street. Room 210."

Roonie knew the place well. "Do you know how much I cost?" she asked, taking control of the conversation for the sake of her own comfort. The security man nodded and prematurely handed her a wad of bills. With nimble fingers she counted them, noting that the full price was paid. Something reeked of fish. "How do you know I just won't show?"

"I know you will." With a wave of his hand, he dismissed her and returned to his multiple screens.

On the elevator ride up, she imagined the hulking man naked, asking her to get on her knees, demanding her full compliance. She thought of Giles, who asked nothing of her but would have received everything from Jonathan. Then, as the elevator dinged, her mind lingered on herself, the giver but never the receiver of anything but green paper.

COMPLEXES

Chapter Five

Morrissey alerted Gerard to the situation—Ruthy was clutching her chest, unable to speak, struggling to breathe. He rushed to his older sister's side, speaking words of false comfort. "Just relax, we'll get you help. Antony! Get a damn car! Call an ambulance!"

His son stood, eyes wide at the doorway, frozen at the sight of Ruthy, an eroding rock. "Y-yeah. Which one? A car? An ambulance?" he shouted back, limbs trembling and brain fizzing out.

"Just call 911!"

Antony nodded and rushed out of his line of vision.

Gerard returned his attention to his sister, who sat on a wooden chair, where she rested after taking a flight of stairs. "Is it your chest, Ruthy?" She faintly moved her head. Guessing she was suffering from a heart attack, he told Morrissey to search for aspirin in the kitchen or bathroom. Shortly she returned, holding all the medication she could carry. Dumping the pill bottles on the floor, Morrissey began picking through her pile for the well-hidden aspirin.

"Here!" she exclaimed, struggling to open the Bayer with her quivering hands. Gerard seized the bottle from her, opened it, and asked Ruthy to chew on it. When she swallowed she gave an audible breath.

CHAPTER FIVE

Antony came pacing into the room, on his cell phone, answering the dispatcher's questions. "Yes. Floor E. Yeah, the floors are lettered, that goes unquestioned! Take the stairs, the elevator's slow. Okay. Dad?" He held out his phone to Gerard, whose arm was draped over his sister, rubbing her shoulder. "Dad, she wants to speak to you."

Taking the phone and speaking with a quavering voice, he said, "Hello? I don't know CPR. Do you, Morrissey?" The girl shook her head, concocting a soft-voiced excuse for her current inadequacy. Gerard continued to converse with the dispatcher, asking for directions on what to do should Ruthy stop breathing.

"Goddamn cigarettes." She regained her raspy voice, though she panted still. At the sound of her voice, Morrissey hugged her worriedly, face planted in her bosom. "Morrissey, don't you dare start smoking," Ruthy managed with a painful sounding cough.

Five excruciatingly long minutes, littered mostly with silence and Ruthy's short breaths, ended in the wail of sirens in the distance. Antony left to meet them at the door of the Complexes, mostly to direct them to the correct floor. Another two minutes passed before he returned, the EMTs in tow. Gerard released his grip on his sister and allowed her to be taken by the EMTs, two women who appeared much more capable than he. Adroitly yet with care, they loaded Ruthy onto a stretcher and began moving her out, occupying the entire elevator this trip.

As Gerard followed the emergency team, he saw in the doorway of her apartment Mara, her hand delicately covering her face. "What happened?" she asked, concerned. "If you need a car, I can drive you to the hospital." Figuring it would be easier to follow in a car than to invade upon the medics' work in the ambulance, Gerard took her up on her offer.

The trio made four took the stairs and walked across the quiet street to the parking garage, where the Speare family car was located. Once Mara started the vehicle, she turned off the coffeehouse music station that was originally playing, leaving them with silence and the engine. "Are they taking her to St. Peter's?" she asked as she drove out of the garage, spotting the howling ambulance. Gerard confirmed, yes, but remained uncharacteristically silent. Part of him wished Mara hadn't witnessed the moment of crisis and offered to help— he felt vulnerable, as if his heart were skipping rope and failing at it.

In the back, Morrissey and Antony were exchanging low words of comfort. After reassuring his cousin that her mother was a tough one, he grasped her head and kissed it playfully, an act of affection so rarely seen that it forced a smile out of Gerard. Mara's sudden brake at the red stoplight brought him back to reality, however. If he lost Ruthy, he would lose the rest of his original family. He'd have to somehow take care of Morrissey, else she'd return to California with his alienated parents. A funeral would have to be arranged, and those parents would be in attendance, for the first time seeing Antony. Antony would probably be furious with him, given that Gerard never gave him the opportunity to know his grandparents or his history. His stay at the Complexes would be cut short if he attempted to escape, and good-bye Mara Speare.

Maybe the last one was a tad more selfish, but in effect, things would go to shit if Ruthy died.

As they disembarked from the car at the hospital's emergency entrance, Mara asked kindly, "Do you want me to stay? Or bring anything while you wait?" As much as he would have enjoyed her company, Gerard refused to keep her from her home. "Let me know how things are when you come back to the Complexes, okay?" She said good-bye with a nervous smile, rolled up her window, and merged into traffic.

In a waiting room they remained, Morrissey in a ball, Antony occupying two seats, and Gerard pacing. After thirty minutes a doctor approached them and informed them that, yes, Ruth Shepherd had suffered a heart attack due to her undiagnosed emphysema. "She smokes a lot," Morrissey told the doctor tearfully. "I told her not to smoke a lot or you'll end up like that man with a hole in his throat in those commercials!" Though the doctor agreed with her sentiment, he stated that drastic measures such as that were not necessary quite yet, that they were working to stabilize her, and that the worst was over.

An hour into the wait, their stomachs and moods began rumbling. Morrissey complained that the doctors in St. Peter's weren't as good as Olympia Medical, where Ruthy infrequently got her checkups. She whined that she was hungry, that if her mother wasn't a smoker she'd be eating dinner right now. Finally, she nagged Antony on the rips on his jeans, calling it "so not classy," just like everything else about him.

Eventually Morrissey nodded asleep, leaving the two in a semblance of peace.

"Dad," Antony anxiously said, "I need to tell you something. It's sort of bad timing, but after that car ride, I figured you'd want to know."

At the mention of the car ride, Gerard guessed the subject of this discussion. "What about Mara?" he asked, her name new on his lips, just like a rush of confidence from new, fitted jeans.

He exhaled. "I had an argument with Angus last week, and ..." He paused, rubbing his nose, then went on. "He said that you were hitting on her and asked you to back off. I defended you, you know, but real shit's going to go down if you continue down that road." Antony then shook his head and said with more verve, "Ah, shit, you're an adult; you don't need a lecture from me. Do whatever the hell you want, Dad. We always can pack up if we mess up, anyway."

Gerard gazed at his son, carefully picking apart his emotions from his troubled eyes and itchy nose. "Tell me the truth: do you want to leave?"

Antony, who had been looking away, faced his father squarely. Tiredly, he confessed, "I never want to leave." He sniffed and focused his eyes on the tile floor again, leaving his father to contemplate what had been exchanged.

Another handful of minutes passed, and other waiters around them joined and left. Morrissey remained asleep and Antony in his zone, while Gerard thought of his sister and of Alice and of Mara. He lived a relatively healthy life, and, save youth rehab, remained out of hospitals. Before Ruthy's heart attack, he had only been to the hospital once before: in Frisco, when Antony was born.

As far as Gerard could see, the solution to his staying-or-leaving problem lay either in abandonment of his pursuit of Mara. Then they could remain in the Complexes, with Ruthy and Morrissey, and hopefully in some sort of harmony with the Speare family.

COMPLEXES

But even if they moved away, he had to settle someplace soon, for Antony soon would turn eighteen and consequently leave him to the dogs to chase his own dreams.

It was a thought that frightened Gerard more than anything else. From a crying baby to a teenage heroin addict to a vagrant adult, he had always had someone to depend on, be it his family or a drug dealer. The very concept of being alone, without a partner or trusty accomplice, left him significantly drained. Ruthy's attack only reminded him of the fleeting nature of life. Antony's disclosure increased his failures by size and influence.

So he had to find someone, and he had less than a year to do it.

The doctor emerged from the forbidding doors again, bearing good news. Ruthy was stabilized, and all, except for her emphysema, was well. Morrissey, who had been awakened by Antony's nudge, burst into thankful tears onto her cousin's shoulder. "Can we see her?" she asked. The doctor agreed, and led them to the room where she slept.

Morrissey cried into the hospital sheets once the doctor walked away. "Mom, you're so stupid! Stupid, stupid, stupid."

Gerard sat behind her, pushed her bangs from her forehead tenderly. "Your mother's not stupid. Perhaps a little naïve, but not stupid."

CHAPTER FIVE

Her red face emerged from the white and said with the wisdom of a child, "Naïve doesn't have the same ring as stupid."

Mara's eyes fluttered open to off-white bedsheets and a gray atmosphere one would not normally expect on a perfectly fine early July morning. Tempted to sleep again, she turned over in bed and inhaled through her nose the familiar aroma of sleep. Nothing, to Mara, rivaled the exhausted trust involved in falling asleep—recently, not even the feeling of falling in love, a phenomenon she hardly remembered.

But of course, beside her the clock beeped, indicating the hour, and James exhaled, reminding her of his presence. His eyes still clamped shut, he turned over, facing her. Mara held her breath for a second, afraid of awakening him. James could be a real grump in the mornings; she, on the other hand, loved dawn and the time associated with it, for it was then she was most productive and chipper. In Calcutta, she and her brothers would rise extra early to catch the garbage trucks depositing the rich people's trash in the dumps, so they could scavenge for recyclables and even valuables. Then, Mara would open up shop and sell whatever they gathered plus some.

She had to wonder what would have become of her had James not plucked her out of her poverty. Her infrequent contact with her siblings suggested that she probably would have been married off to as rich a person as would accept her hand, none richer than James himself. All things considered, she should be glad to live in a somewhat stable household, with a once successful man, with two intelligent sons.

Still, a good chunk of her yearned for India, now more than ever.

While in Italy, she'd never imagined that her blissful journey would end as a lonely housewife. In Italy, she smelled the pheromones literally radiating from James, who taught her how to kiss and how to dance and how to look pensive while looking at art. "I want to marry you," he said, forehead brushed against hers in a passionate moment while in Santa Felicita, Florence. She gleefully reciprocated, and they found a chapel and got the whole thing done without another word to their families.

The entire trip to Italy was directly out of a dream sequence. After they first made love, she swirled her fingers across her chest in tiny circles and asked him to pinch her. James pinched her, kissed her, and convinced her that for this moment, everything was real. "I do love you," he confessed, sticking in an extra word to assure her of his sincerity.

Mara responded in a similar fashion, with a whitened smile and westernized clothes on her back. While he taught her love, he also included free language classes, often times literally drilling her Bengali speech habits from her mouth. She sold her saris to an exotic shop and purchased fine jewelry that as a child she wished she would find shimmering in the dumps. "I want to see the large world you've seen," she said. "I want to see Australia."

Though she learned many things, she found herself a teacher as well. James had yet to grow into his philanthropic parents' shoes, as he most often cared for himself exclusively. To remedy this, Mara related anecdotes of her childhood, from watching childbirth to escaping the clutches of a drunken, dangerous man. She watched him soften at this, for because his precious gem had previously been sullied by poverty, he had an obligation to aid those in the same position she once was in. She taught him how to be gentle, not to crush with his strong grip but to find equilibrium in a handshake.

Many of these things, she guessed, had been forgotten. With the back of her hand she gingerly brushed James's face, felt his body heat exuding from him. There Mara lingered, arm extended, wondering if Italy was in his dreams at all.

She rose from bed, contemplating a hearty breakfast for the two men left in the house. Giles had left weeks ago, silently towing away his garbage bags full of clothes and belongings the dead of night. Since then, Mara and James had moved from their

COMPLEXES

expandable bed in the living room to Giles's old room. Occupying it felt wrong in her bones, for she wished that this change would only be impermanent. Every night she fell asleep knowing it wasn't.

Mara switched on the stove, poured vegetable oil into a pan, and counted five eggs for the morning meal. As the eggs and bacon cooked, she prepared pancake mix sprinkled with chocolate chips. The aroma inevitably drew James, who shuffled from the room, eyes still drooped. He acknowledged his wife with a nod and seated himself at the table, resting his head in his hands.

Biting the urge to say something more provocative, Mara settled with, "Can you wake Angus? I don't want him to oversleep this summer." James complied, but instead of getting up and knocking on his boy's door, he simply called him harshly. She glared at him over her shoulder for the literal rude awakening; he pretended he didn't notice.

Ten minutes later, after the eggs were done cooking and one pancake was flipped, Angus trudged from his room, his brown hair sticking up in strange places. Yawning into his hand, he greeted his mother with a nod and plopped down haphazardly at the table, phone in tow. Underneath the table, he texted that unknown person he always contacted.

CHAPTER FIVE

"Let's put away the phone at the table," James ordered firmly as his son's fingers rapidly flew across the touch screen. Angus began texting over the table as an act of defiance before locking his phone and lightly slamming it on the wood without a look at his father. Incensed, James questioned, "What's with the attitude?"

Angus crossed his arms and slouched down on his chair. "What attitude?" he retorted, his grumpiness showing.

Mara shook her head over the pancakes, flipping another one; the two were so alike at times that they simply did not mix. She couldn't remember at what point Angus started purposefully provoking his father—perhaps sixth grade? What event had triggered their infernal dislike for each other, she was unaware. No matter—it sickened her and fueled an intense dislike for situations wherein the two of them were in the same room. Mara loved her mornings, but her family preferred their lonely evenings, evidently.

"Don't be rude to me or your mother. You know I don't like phones at the table," James slowly stated, in an attempt to be reasonable.

"I dunno, *Father*," Angus said, mocking the formal term James insisted his sons employ. "Some things you've just got to live with."

Leaning forward at the table, like a panther prepared to pounce, James said, "If you're talking about Giles, no, in fact, I did not have to live with him."

"I never asked you to kick him out!" Angus's palms thudded against the tabletop.

"I don't know, Angus," Mara interjected, for she knew that Angus's behavior too often contradicted his words. "You were never thrilled whenever your brother came home anyway." She recalled the laundry event, that searing moment when it seemed she'd have to choose between having her son and pushing him away, all because of Angus's challenging words.

The boy stood up, furious. "Stop ganging up on me. I never asked for Giles to leave—and now he's gone for good all thanks to you." Angus strode away, leaving his stinging words on Mara's ears. A pancake burned before she could flip it over. James, who stood when Angus did, adjusted his chair and settled down into it, shrugging off the incident like nothing.

"Why did you have to start that?" Mara had to ask him, turning off the stove with her unsteady fingers. She deposited the final pancake onto the plate but refused to sit down at the table that started it all.

"Angus was being disrespectful," replied James matter-of-factly, like a scientist reciting the elements.

She heard the hostility in her own voice when she finally burst forth from her timidity, "For future reference, what isn't disrespectful to you, James? Did Giles do something you didn't find respectful and that's why you kicked him out? Sometimes I think"—Mara stopped, finding herself surprisingly short of breath, and weakly finished—"that he was right in leaving."

Silence ensued. She was certain that Angus had his ear to his bedroom door, listening in. James, in a voice that almost sounded broken, said, "Do you really think that way?" More angrily, more frantically, he persisted, "Tell me you really believe what you just said, Mara."

Well—she swallowed—did she? Just this morning Mara considered transcending time to prevent her from ever agreeing to Italy in the first place. But with everything she held dear at stake, could she just walk away for her own, selfish peace of mind? "No," she admitted, both to James and herself. "I would never leave. But Giles was right."

Incredulously, James said, "How is he right?"

Clamping her eyes shut and clutching the plate of pancakes with both hands, she replied firmly, "He just is, and your stubbornness is not helping the case."

"So you and Angus both are siding with him." He pointed toward the door, through the walls and into the treacherous E07.

"There are no sides here."

"Like hell there aren't!"

COMPLEXES

Mara jumped, her grip failed, and the dish bounced off the ground and seemed to shatter in midair, leaving the pancakes piled on the tiled floor. She couldn't remembered the last time James had roared like that, if he ever had at all. Kneeling down, she, as cautiously as she could manage with her trembling hands, picked up the pieces of the broken plate. In her distress, Mara hardly heard the footsteps of her husband walking away.

Even if Giles was right, she had too much of a heart to leave. Now, Mara was the only one remaining, cutting the tips of her fingers on the fragments left behind.

Jonathan hadn't ordered shark fin soup—he wouldn't have, even if he knew Giles enjoyed it so much. Either Mano had somehow wriggled himself into their movie-watching tradition or Giles had invited him. It was easier on Jonathan's mind to believe the former. "Whose funky idea was this?" the shark, who was more like a muscled blue teddy bear, asked. Giles confirmed that it was his, and Mano ceased to comment on the absurdity of it all. *He couldn't possibly understand the way Giles's mind works*, figured Jonathan spitefully. *Not in the way that I do.*

CHAPTER FIVE

After popping in the movie, the muscled blue teddy bear had the stuffed nerve to sit in between Jonathan and the cross-legged Giles, with his arm slung across the couch, dangerously close to Giles's shoulder. Robbed of intimacy, Jonathan proceeded to focus, hard, on the movie— focus on the movie, not the way the television light illuminated Giles's face like a neon artwork.

The Game, the movie was called, at least according to the minimalist title screen of white letters and black background. The words faded out, gradually revealing a man sitting at a computer and chewing on his lip. In a manner that revealed the monstrosity of it all, he arose, took a knife, and stabbed his younger sister as she ran up a flight of stairs. Grueling was a good word to describe it, although Mano had exclaimed, "Cool," and inched his arm closer to Giles.

The man, Daniel, escaped the house by means of a heavily tattooed girl in a pickup truck. They discussed in low voices a game they both played, the very game that set Daniel with the task of murdering his sister. After experiencing a change of heart, the murderer decided to seek revenge upon the master of the game, named Triple A. "This is confusing," Mano remarked. "If he didn't want to kill his sister, why did he do it in the first place?"

"The primal need to win," answered Giles, who, out of the corner of Jonathan's eye, appeared to be deeply immersed in the convoluted film. "They're playing a game, and he wanted to win. What he was going to win ... salvation, pride, boasting rights."

"He's not going to get it now that he wants revenge, though," Jonathan piped in, refusing to be blockaded from the conversation by Mano's big mouth. "I say if you're going to do something, don't regret it afterwards."

"You're one to talk."

He inwardly winced. This little debate was another one of Giles's games. Even with a third party in the room, he persisted in piercing tender spots with his spear-like words. Giles continued, "As for the salvation, he'll get it in his own way."

"Have you seen this before?" Mano interjected.

For the first time, his eyes ripped off the television set and turned to Mano. "No."

Mano chuckled into his words. "You're weird." His arm slid from the couch and playfully knocked the side of Giles's head. "I like that about you." He received a hint of a smile in return. Jonathan loudly cleared his throat, averting his attention from the subtle flirting back to the movie.

Daniel hid with the woman and her oblivious yet warmhearted brother. With the help of a hacker he contacted during his stay, he discovered the location of Triple A's computer. Weaved into the plot were tiny bits of Daniel's past. The Game—a game where listless people find a purpose, a goal—had changed his life. One flashback showed Daniel's murdering a rabbit and his sister crying over the discovered animal's corpse.

"Jesus, why would anyone want to kill a rabbit for some points in a game?" Mano wondered. Jonathan waited for Giles to respond (as he wanted no deep discourse with the shark), but he remained silent. Something within that scene had resonated within Giles. Perhaps Jonathan would learn of it later, but for now, the ignorant two contributed to the silence.

The hacker directed Daniel to a drugstore. Inside, he found that woman who had helped him, pointing a gun at him. At that moment, he knew that that not so oblivious, not so warmhearted brother of hers was Triple A. The Game master himself made an appearance. As the hacker had informed the police, they had little time for conversation. They debated, yelled abstractly about the meaning of life and the meaning of the Game. In the end, the sister joined the ranks of Cain, and Daniel took the gun and became Triple A.

Mano's loud voice overshadowed the quiet epilogue. "Wait, what? Why'd he bite the bullet?" Giles patiently answered all of his questions, leaving Jonathan to contemplate the strange film alone. He understood the gist of it—life consists of tiny tasks. Which tasks are mandated to you and which tasks are of your own choice? What happens when people make a choice to have tasks mandated to them? Do you lose your free will? Will a perfect world emerge out of a community of devotees? Daniel, in effect, became Triple A to save the brother and sister from jail. Was it his choice or was it Triple A's suicide mission all along?

After all his less provocative questions were answered, Mano stood up to stretch his legs. "Well, I think we should go now." In a quiet manner that revealed the awkwardness of it all, Giles also arose, took his cell phone, and promised to call Jonathan later. Without another word, Jonathan watched the couple slide out the door, into oblivion.

Was Jonathan letting Giles go or was he mandated to let him go? Did Giles choose to leave or was he mandated to leave?

He slapped his cheeks and shivered. It was too damn cold to think about shit like that, but he thought of it anyway. They were probably in Mano's apartment or out on the city, drinking and pretending to be adult like. Jonathan could imagine Giles tearing open his wounds and allowing the shark to follow the scent. After luring Mano close enough, Giles killed him and prepared shark fin soup with his genitals.

Any daydream in which Giles sucked wet dicks made Jonathan uncomfortable and unhappy and hard and yet so unaroused. And yet, he hoped that Giles would devour him, absorb his being until there was nothing left. Maybe the excess of blue hair would make him want red.

When Jonathan woke up the next morning, Giles still hadn't returned. While sleep still numbed his heart, he listened to the voicemail left on his phone.

"Good. You're sleeping. I just wanted to tell you. It's belated, but feelings were … reciprocated. What does Martha call it? We're going steady? *Ha-ha.* Well. Sweet dreams, Nathan."

The phone felt unfamiliar in his clammy hands. Jonathan slapped his cheeks, hoping for remnants of motivation, but his hands remained on his face. He began to cry.

One monotonous month passed after Ruthy returned from the hospital, and Antony had bored himself to an out-of-body state. He'd sit like a vegetable in designated spots, attempting to pipe up conversations with his dwindling list of acquaintances: Morrissey and Sans. His other two friends weren't speaking to him right now—Angus, because of parental drama, and Jessie, simply because she never seemed to be around. Occasionally he'd pass her in the hallway; they'd exchange cordial greetings but never anything more than that. Last he saw her, she looked a little gaunt.

The weather was equally down, with temperatures below freezing. He'd have ventured the city and make friends like a bee collects pollen if it weren't for the unsunny weather. Upon asking Sans how he sat in the security room watching shadows of people pass by all day, he received a nonchalant "I get paid to do it, I get paid." The frost bit at his smoky hands when he occasionally bummed a cig outside the Complexes (for every day was becoming like one of those days). He'd wait just as he waited for Angus at an indistinct door, inhaling until he made himself dizzy with nicotine.

"That's bad for your health," Gerard would say dumbly as he handed his son another pack of cigarettes.

"I know, I should quit," said Antony to himself as he lit up again. Originally, he was a social smoker, then a waiting-for-people smoker. Now, as a waiting-for-nobody smoker, he felt too much like his father, too busy chasing the coattails of the past, too busy looking for something that wasn't going to be there. Angus was E floors away—he could simply formulate an apology during the slow elevator ride. The thought made Antony chuckle; apologizing for nothing just wasn't his style. He wasn't that desperate for companionship. He could happily deal on his own.

Well, he thought that many times. The truth embedded somewhere inside him pleaded for the one thing he hardly had: stability. Antony took a sharp inhale at the return of the "s" word. On easier days, his father could serve as that unwavering structure, when he wasn't being a strange romantic hypocrite playing with shadow-like dust bunnies. It was like when Antony came to Gerard drinking and drunk for the first time at age fourteen, and Gerard began drinking to be drunk with him. What he wanted was a decent scolding. He received an unromantic scene that included snipped blond hair and box cutters and, of course, the medium of the culprit, intoxicating substances. Antony awoke the next day with hair that spiked and a feeling that his jaw resembled his father's far too much.

Thoughts tend to recur when you repeat the same movements day by day, or so Antony discovered after he finished his penultimate cigarette. It hit him like high tide on a blue moon that he would be like his father as long as he made the same mistakes, mistakes probably human and understandable but otherwise unknown.

It was unfair to him, truly, to be the product of a nomad. He had the ability to defend his background against anyone but himself. And angst, though unlike him, came as easily as hunger.

Such thoughts circulated his racetrack mind as Antony tapped the end of his cigarette against the bottom of his shoe. He returned to the Complexes, his gloved hand barely touching the banister as he trudged up the stairs. His life consisted of more starts and restarts than the average person's, and, he figured, they'd run out of time.

But of course, life would pitch one more curveball to make him rethink.

Antony, framed by the doorway, hand on the knob, rested his eyes on his father. Gerard's arms, wrapped around Mara, didn't budge, but his shoulders trembled as he breathed. Mara's back was to Antony; she wept audibly and didn't notice his presence. The look on Gerard's face was fool's gold.

Antony averted his eyes from the illegal embrace and shut the door lightly. His gloved hand brushed the freezing banister as he allowed gravity to tug him down the stairs one heavy foot at a time. He squashed his last cigarette with a stomp that sounded nothing like the ultimatum he'd formed in his mind.

Yes, he knew, they'd run out of time.

She was walking, and then she was on the bridge. The lapse of memory, though inaccurate, seemed more fitting to Jessie, and could she describe that to the evaluator and get away with a slap on the sliced wrist, she'd gladly do it. But it simply wasn't right, for there were moments when she felt the concrete bounce back like rubber as she walked wobbly lines toward an equally unsure destination. Cars swooshed past her, causing her hair to stand up on multiple ends—or was it the fear? Either way, she ascended a few steps, pulled her skirt down to unsuccessfully hide her goose bumps and scars from herself, and continued on the length of the bridge. She had walked a little past the middle before pausing, slipping her shoes off her feet and her bag off her shoulder. One leg over the railing. Two legs over the railing.

Immediately, Jessie felt dizzy and alone and cold, save her eyes, hot with tears, which focused on the crashing river below her. Later, lying in the hospital bed with her mother crying, she failed to remember what, exactly, she was thinking in that moment. A will to die, yes, that was undeniable—but she wanted someone to save her, too.

More cars zoomed by, cars full of people who didn't notice the girl standing awkwardly, leaning toward a watery abyss. Vaguely, she recalled Hilde describing the river that was, once, a fantasy escape hatch. "Is it the cold that draws you, the freezing water?" she asked.

"No," Jessie said, "it's because I can't swim."

Why now? Why this fear, at this particular moment, when she had the stomach to go this far? Death dies eventually; death is only a transition point, a tunnel, the fall. Ah, but the fall includes the water, and the water is composed of fear. To quote from a blog of teenagers phasing from emo to hipster, she was too afraid to live and too afraid to die.

All this she stupidly figured in ten minutes. Eventually she crouched down, hands sticking to the railing, knees knocking each other, her chin, her teeth. "Fuck it," she chattered aloud, slowly straightening her bent limbs. *I'll come back when I'm intoxicated out of my mind or something else that will probably never happen.*

"Are you okay?"

Goddamnit, just when she had surrendered to life. But the presence of a fellow human being, hand outstretched, eyes a little panicky, was enough to make the tears in her eyes spring forth and transform her from a logical yet suicidal young woman into a blubbering, unintelligible little girl.

The man grabbed Jessie's arm, holding it with both hands. His fingers were warm. Hours later Jessie would attempt to piece together features of the man's face. Ultimately, all she remembered was that hold he had on her, one hand holding hers, one hand beyond her elbow, as if he were aiming her arm like a shotgun. "What's your name? My name is Nick. What's your name?"

"Jessie," she sniffed.

Very calmly, he continued, "Good. Jessie. How old are you?"

"Sixteen."

"Okay, Jessie. Did you take anything? Drugs? Heroin, cocaine?" Aside, to another

CHAPTER FIVE

man who had appeared seemingly out of nowhere, "Call the police."

She shook her head. "I want to … I want to…" *I want to go home!*

"You'll be fine, Jessie. Just come over here." Weakly, she nodded, and with his support she gauchely climbed the railing and collapsed, bare legs scraping the concrete. With the man's guidance, she edged herself to the curb and sat there, curled, shoes and bag abandoned on the windy bridge. Within minutes, a police car came. The men, the same men you see on weekends cursing at football games, checked Jessie's bag for her ID and asked her varying questions about her background. After calling the ambulance, the police drove away to contact Jessie's parents. The man with bad timing, the man who the police said "saved" her, had disappeared among the sirens and flashing lights.

The entire charade was like smoke and mirrors to Jessie. Somehow, she convinced herself that she was going home, not to a hospital where they would poke and prod her and admit her to an inpatient program. She was okay. She had just about given up on suicide anyway when that man with bad timing and that warm grip grabbed her.

What's more, she was sorry for her actions. She was sorry the instant other people outside of her normal support group got involved. She was sorry she was a bother to that man, and she was sorry when she saw the expression on her parents' faces when they entered the emergency room.

"Oh why, babe," her mother sobbed into the blanket.

Jessie's eyebrows hurt from scrunching up so much. Her eyes, already small, were all swollen up. "I don't know, Mom. I wish I could tell you."

This she told her evaluator; the evaluator, with her long white hair and unsympathetic thick glasses, admitted her to inpatient once again. Her parents left to retrieve clothes for her extended stay at the Olympia Medical Adolescent Inpatient Program. Hours passed in the waiting room before strange nurses who were used to swollen, wide eyes guided her through heavy locked double doors into her new room. It was two in the morning when she collapsed on an itchy bed with only one unfortunately flat pillow, her stranger of a roommate sleeping soundly on the other side of the room.

The next morning, she heard the familiar phrase, "Male in the female wing. Get up, ladies. Time to wake up."

Time to wake up, Jessie.

Chapter Six

The cold opened its mouth and gave way to a snowy August. It was in this transitioning of months when Angus discovered one of the pharmacy's frequenters was HIV positive. The sheepish, timid young man handed him a brand new prescription for AZT. The patron kept his eyes trained on the carpeted ground. "Are you waiting for the prescription or coming back for it?" Angus asked his repertoire of questions steadily.

"Right, yeah, I'll just buy a lottery ticket." He shot Angus a charming smile that reminded him of Giles.

In those fifteen minutes, after awkwardly frequenting the rows of the pharmacy five times, James approached him. They exchanged a few low words; Angus strained his ears to listen. "You wouldn't happen to know my son? You're about the same age and—"

The young man frowned a little, shook his head. "No, I don't, sir…?"

James stole a look around the pharmacy, occupied by a few patients awaiting their prescriptions, and his eyes collided with the eavesdropping Angus'. He gestured his head over to the back room; the two continued the conversation behind those closed doors. They emerged a few minutes later, the conversation having achieved its mysterious purpose. The man picked up his prescription and left; James looked as proud and spiteful as ever.

The night and business slowed, and Angus left the pharmacy early to go home and hibernate underneath a galaxy thick pile of blankets. His mind was plagued by that young man with a charming smile who possibly knew Giles and was HIV positive and was kind looking. The possible red string between HIV and his brother encircled his chest in the barbed wire of anxiety.

Angus sidestepped into a nearby Starbucks, hoping to replace his well-earned money with a warm drink between his hands. He couldn't help but notice a familiar streak of curly red in the early evening hubbub – and he ordered an extra peppermint mocha with his own chai latte under the name of Jonathan.

Aforementioned streak of curly red confusedly looked up at the barista's peal. Angus retrieved the drinks and slid deftly into the seat across from him. Jonathan's mouth opened dumbly at the sight of a kindly Angus. The two freshly brewed drinks steamed before them, untouched. "What is it?" Jonathan inquired, "A consolation present for your being an asshole?"

"Can we just," Angus cleared his throat and encircled hands around his latte, "start over?"

CHAPTER SIX

Jonathan considered this for only a mere second before taking the proffered drink and gulping it down. "You've got as long as this drink lasts to convince me."

"I'm not looking to convince," he responded, endeavoring to maintain a level head. "Are you tested for HIV?"

He spluttered, wasting precious time and precious drink. "How is that any of your business?"

"If you're sleeping with my brother—"

"—I already told you that I'm not—"

"—I just want him to be okay." Angus paused, inhaled shakily, and put his hypothesis to a test. "My dad and I just want him to be okay."

Licking his chapped lips, Jonathan gazed sideways and downwards. "Look, I haven't slept with anyone, including Giles, since I met him. Last I was tested, I don't have HIV." His eyes then closed, as though accepting judgment. "I wish I could say I kept a good eye on him. Right now, he's dating another man."

Disappointment tempted Angus's anger, but he remained quiet. The Starbucks table had transformed into a confessional when Angus finally managed, "I'm sorry for calling you a fucking faggot. Please believe me when I say homophobic isn't the right word to describe me; I'm not afraid or hateful towards you. Maybe towards my brother, but not you."

"I understand." Jonathan nodded vaguely, though his mind was already elsewhere. "I feel—I feel horrible, you know." His fingers hid his freckled face as he exhaled extensively.

Angus admitted, recalling the argument about the un-fresh cookies, "It's not your fault; we did this to ourselves, but I can't forgive you."

Jonathan slapped the heat back into his cheeks. "I get that you can't. I'd keep apologizing if it made everything okay." He extended a gloved hand, an armistice. "I wish your family the best."

"What's left of it." He accepted Jonathan's hand despite his own lingering bitterness. After shaking hands and emptying their cups, they walked in the same direction toward the Complexes, discussing the weather. August, now just as cold, as February, looked unfortunately bleak. "It's not going to get warmer, is it?" Angus asked, his frosted breath floating between them.

They thought nothing of the police car parked on the curb in front of the Complexes. Angus, however, took note when the elevator doors slid open, revealing a pair of policemen at the door of E02. Instantly, his thoughts fled from his thawing nose to his hot heart, to Jessie. "What happened?" The words dropped from his mouth like a leak from a faucet. Louder, he repeated, "What happened?"

The men turned, shot Angus an anxious look. Marie stepped, albeit weakly, from E02, coat on and keys in her hand, the bags under her eyes weighing her entire face down. "It's all right," she assured the cops, herself, and Angus, all at once with an unsure voice. "Please, Angus, I'll tell you later."

Unconvinced, more urgently, Angus said, "Is Jessie okay, Mrs. Rivera?"

She sniffed a good three times, fumbling her keys with her trembling fingers. "Please," she insisted, "call me Tita. And Jessie, Jessie is fine."

Angus released the breath he was holding. Jonathan placed his hand on his shoulder, beckoning his head towards E01. "I'll see you later." To Marie, he gave a toothy grin and a "It's nice to meet you."

Angus had to pick his jaw up from the floor before he awkwardly sidestepped the police and Marie to get to his apartment. Mara looked up abruptly when he walked in and leaned against the closed door. "What happened?" she asked, sounding like an ironic broken record.

He remembered when he first saw Jessie, and was thoroughly unimpressed. She looked funny with her dyed hair and growing black roots. But when she opened her mouth, she tried so damn hard to be like those girls in those books who mean something and—and he took pity on her. That pity transmuted with the elements of sensitivity, lust, and awe to become what he felt for her today.

COMPLEXES

Somehow he knew that this concept of Jessie would change. Something died just now; the police probably arrested it and sentenced it to a life term. She would no longer be a girl with a pixie cut and a past that he was interested in. She had singlehandedly brought their relationship to the point of no return, the point where commitment was required.

Honestly, Angus was afraid. Commitment, as far as he was concerned, led to brewing domestic trouble or starstruck gazes that caused brewing domestic trouble. And yet commitment was what he longed for—a long-term dream achieved, perhaps even an extended romance. But once you put crying mothers and policemen in the hallway, you know serious shit has come to crash in your apartment.

He could spend the rest of the night wondering what happened and what would happen and how he would handle it. But the thought of Antony Shepherd appeared like a crop circle in his far-reaching mind. His stupid smile and his vagrant dreams reminded him of their conversations at the Chouette Chouette, over the food they ordered on a whim.

CHAPTER SIX

As the nights grew longer like unkempt weeds in the summer, Rooney found herself trembling in bed, listening to but not hearing NPR, constantly climbing up and down the stairs from floor E to the streets to smoke a cigarette. Something magnificent grated at her nerves. Dizziness and anticipation for the unknown, perhaps? A beer-bellied man had now castled his rooks and king during a game she didn't know she was playing. There were people in the world Rooney thought she would never sleep with: the security guard was one of them.

Purse heavy with lingerie, she walked, heels clicking along the recently rinsed midnight sidewalk. Before entering that hotel on Lafayette and Church Street, she smoked until her head became as light as the balloons that carried the little boy away in that charming French movie. Counting her breaths and seemingly counting the times her hands shook this way and that, she bowed her head in acknowledgement to the half-asleep doorman and entered. Far too used to disregarding the elevator, Rooney took a flight of stairs to the second floor. The hallways seemed to wind as decorative walls gave into plush floors. Finally, she arrived at room 201.

Rooney knocked, eyes on the peephole. The man on the other side could squint through and into her soul. Perhaps he would see how racked she was. Perhaps he would have pity. More likely, he would be aroused.

This was far from her first time. Hell, she was used to the process. Open the door, politely introduce yourself, laugh behind your hand around the awkward innuendoes, and then go into the bathroom to make final adjustments. But her instinct warned her against it, so severely that the fear on her face shined through a thin veneer of sweat, despite the cold.

The door opened. The security guard was there, dressed in large-fitting suit and tie. "Hello," was all he said, in such a chipper tone that it penetrated her ears like a snake invading a rabbit hole. "I'm afraid I've been rude. I haven't introduced myself properly. I'm Sans."

"Sans," she responded, in what she hoped sounded like a low and sexy voice, "it's a pleasure to see you again, after so long a wait." She wanted to throw up; he didn't seem to notice.

"Please, come in." She complied, and her heels sunk into another fancy layer of carpet. Sans started speaking—to Rooney he might as well have been reciting Mother Goose poems—and stared at her, eyes twinkling with eagerness, akin to a young boy receiving a new video game. Rooney wanted to scream—*I'm not a game; I'm not a toy!*—but she managed to laugh behind her hand and comment on what he said without really adding to the conversation.

CHAPTER SIX

Her insides churned. She gestured to the bathroom, whose door was ajar. "May I?" she asked before sliding into the temporary safe haven. The bathroom lights were so white they nearly blinded her. Her stomach boiled. She spent a good ten minutes hugging her arms around the toilet, staring into the drainage as if deciphering a fortune in tea. Saliva gathered in her mouth, and her bowels seemed to move into her throat.

Although her internal pep talk didn't heal her nausea, the moments of silence did. She blamed it on the cigarettes and stood up, undressed herself, and redressed in pretty white lingerie. Bleakly, she shot a final look in the mirror. Gorgeous, yes, gaunt for some men's tastes, but gorgeous. She stepped into her high-heeled shoes and exited, one foot a little diagonal from the other to accentuate her curves. Sans was sitting on the couch, hands on his knees, eyes on her. "Do you like it?" she asked, pausing in her walk and placing her hand on her cocked hip.

"Admittedly, yes," he said, chuckling. "But I think this suits you more." Rooney deflated a little; picky patrons were always the most enthusiastic, and sometimes the roughest.

Sans opened a closet, then brandished a dark blue dress. It was more conservative than Rooney was used to: knee length, with a small black belt cinching the waist and a V-neck that didn't stoop too deeply. "If you want me to wear it, I will,"

COMPLEXES

Rooney said, extending her hand to receive the dress.

Ignoring her, Sans went on. "I see you in this dress sometimes. In someplace fancy, someplace far from here. Probably in London or Paris—I don't know much about Europe, only that they have fancy restaurants where young women like you wear nice blue dresses and flirt with men in suits and ties over—I don't know—escargots?" He laughed at the amusing word. "Escargots."

"I can do that," Rooney responded with an edge of impatience. If he wanted to role-play, he could have just said that in the first place.

Even in the dim light, his eyes still shone with that stupid anticipation. "Yes, you can. At least, now you can, now you can."

After the dress emerged from the closet came a suitcase, a suitcase that was a treasure chest in disguise. When Sans opened it, a sea of green lay before her.

And gorgeous, gaunt Rooney felt silly and small like a girl. Sans didn't want sex with her. Sans didn't want anything from her at all except a few choice decisions:

"Take the money. Wear the dress when you go to those fancy restaurants in—I don't know—London or Paris. Do something but what you're doing now. Go."

She exhaled, and every pound of strength within her left with her breath, including her resistance. Questions bubbled in the same boiling stomach, but only steam exited her. Rooney took the money. She pulled a trench coat over her exposed body and barely remembered her purse as she left room 201.

"Don't thank me," Sans said. His words were laced hard melancholy, tough love, a concept Rooney only knew the half of. "Just go."

And she went, the suitcase weighing her right side down as she walked along the recently dried midnight sidewalk.

Only once in a blue moon did Giles have nightmares. Dreams about Finch didn't quite count, as they only left him clammy, not drenched in sweat. But tonight, albeit different, felt like a curse in the coming. Giles jerked up and gave out a loud whimper, one so pathetic that T. S. Eliot would think he was dying. "Shit." He shuddered and covered his face with his two hands, inhaling the scent of his smoky fingers.

"Dude." Mano turned over in his sleep and opened one eye. "You okay?" Giles nodded faintly. His boyfriend rolled back, buried his face in his pillow, fauxhawk facing up, and tumbled into slumber. In times like these, Giles really needed a more considerate man.

COMPLEXES

Abandoning any attempt to sleep, Giles slipped out of bed and padded on his bare feet to Mano's tiny balcony, set in a nicer part of town than the Complexes. Elbows on the banister, he lit a cigarette and contemplated the full moon and his nightmare, both of which receded into the clouds.

During times like these and more, he entertained the thought of his being with Jonathan. Jonathan was the unlikely factor in Giles's family drama, thus making his life more difficult yet more enjoyable. Though Giles could blame his behavior on rebellious anger, he also realistically could blame it on funny love. He loved flirting then drawing back, like a cat half playing. Then again, he knew he had been playing this precarious game for too long—with Jonathan and with his family. It was only a matter of time until both gave up.

Nights like these, Giles regretted every movement, every word from his mouth, every push away. For fear that he would be abandoned, he did the abandoning. It was messed up and passive-aggressive and self-hateful, but he did it anyway. He was becoming used to these hazardous relationships, the toxicity of it all.

He supposed it began long ago, when his father would bring Giles to work on "bring your kid to work day" instead of Angus. Whenever the younger brother was scolded, denied praise, the older would come to Angus and attempt to teach him that a father's love wasn't the key to happiness. Still, he suffered from James's lack of emotional sensibility—and Mara did, too.

Mara, Giles's beautiful mother, had begun falling out of love when the brothers were young. James seemed overwhelmed by fatherhood, by married life, as if providing the ring brought no consequences. Instead of addressing his emotions by using his wife as a sounding board, instead of loving, he drew back. Giles, as perceptive as ever, saw that.

And here he was, doing the exact same thing.

"I think I love you." Those were the words Giles overheard their first night in the Complexes. "I moved here for you. Please, let me meet you." As much as he strained his ears, he couldn't hear the words said on the other end of the line. That James was cheating didn't surprise him. That he could express emotions to another human being frightened him.

So Giles let him talk to the mystery person on the phone. He would have his own vengeance. He wouldn't let his father ruin his family.

And his twisted revenge played out strangely, beginning with his own steps, distancing himself in the way he should have long ago. His family needed to stop pretending that everything was okay. If it took him a few drinks with a redhead, so be it.

He began his nights with Jonathan searching for some form of fulfillment, only to find that he was in all probability, bisexual, in love, and frightened to admit it. What would it mean to his family, who was, as far as he knew, thoroughly homophobic, if he officially settled himself with Jonathan? Jonathan was obviously head over heels, but Giles couldn't bring himself to reciprocate. It was terrifying to him, the concept of gaining someone to lose. It was also terrifying to look in the mirror and see more of his father in himself than ever.

So Giles smoked another cigarette and slowly told himself that, yes, he had problems, and his recent promiscuity didn't help. Mano was great in bed, oddly affectionate, and didn't care about Giles's personal life. The little sparks of mindless freedom with Mano had him half convinced there was a life out there for him, outside the clutches of the Speares, and outside of the concept of "true love."

He exhaled a cloud of smoke and returned to the bedside, where Mano slept, far more peacefully than he ever could. Giles leaned over and gently kissed the back of his blue head, breathing in his unfamiliar scent and unconsciously pretending it was Jonathan.

And he knew then that he would never stop having nightmares of losing the people he loved. Never would he have anyone else like Jonathan, Angus, Mara, and James. And he would never be like his father—never.

"Sorry, tough guy," Giles said lowly as he withdrew from the bed. "I have to go home." He was kind, so he left a note before he left. Shivering, he walked the far length home, until dawn arrived in its red-purple glory.

Mara had fallen into his arms like a twittering bird with a broken wing. It was wonderful—she was beautiful, and for a night she'd practice being his—but it was heartbreaking—she was weeping, and was so soft around the edges that she might feather away. Gerard knew that her sudden affections for him were spurred on by a bout of desperation, not by true love.

"Do you want to talk about it?" Gerard asked his son the night he walked in on their strange embrace.

The moment must have looked much more passionate than it really was. In truth, Mara knocked on his door, asked for a conversation over tea, and ended up wordlessly crying her way into Gerard's arms. Not once did Gerard feel as though she truly looked at him. He pretended to be okay with that.

"No," Antony responded, his mind clearly elsewhere.

194

COMPLEXES

Gerard sighed and scratched his head, hoping to show his son that he was, indeed, confused. Despite his being bent on keeping his mouth shut, when Mara entered in her beautiful distress, all determination dropped like an anvil out the window.

"Do you love me, Gerard?"

She was stunning, even with a quivering lip. Her brown eyes overflowed.

Thinking of Alice, he told her yes.

And now he was here, walking Mara to a dinner at the Relais d'Auvergne, a quaint restaurant that once thrived in the summer, as French cafés often do. She wore her long hair in a loose bun, a white skirt that danced around her knees, and a carefree smile that might have suited her had she been younger. Gerard preferred her happy over crying, of course, but still her expression felt ... forced.

Instead of sitting across from him she sat close beside him, arm brushing and fingers intertwining. She talked animatedly about the books she'd been reading, that art history class that she'd been yearning to take online. "I feel young again when I'm with you," she admitted with a practiced blush.

"Look who's here." Of all people in the world to leave Gerard mortified, the second worst appeared. Giles Speare, grinning devilishly, approached, a tall blue-haired man in tow. He was as thin-waisted as a dancing Michael Jackson, and his hair,

CHAPTER SIX

once slightly shaggy, was cleanly cut to a chic pompadour. He invited himself and his date to sit across from the two, despite how visible Gerard made his protests. Mara's flirtatious edge died a hard death as well, as she stopped clinging like moss to Gerard's side.

Giles descended into one-sided small talk, as Mano, who shortly realized who, exactly, they were sitting across from, became equally uncomfortable. "I love it here, don't you? Genuine French cuisine without the—ah—genuine French price. Nice choice for a not too expensive date. Not to criticize—looks like Mano and I wanted something on the cheaper side, too." He rested his chin on his hand, allowing a slow smile to spread across his face.

His mother crossed her legs and pursed her lips, attempting to look preoccupied with the menu. Mano glanced at Gerard, making a hilariously frightened face. Noticing the obvious lull in discourse, Gerard stammered, "Yeah, I've been here once or twice before. I've never been to France, though, so I wouldn't know about genuine—"

"Oh no, I've never been to France either." Giles rapidly picked up on the conversation, leaving no breathing room for Gerard. "But my mother has. Isn't that right?"

"A long, long time ago," Mara confirmed, closing her menu with a swish and focusing her eyes on her son. "The hair's new. Is that what all the boys are sporting nowadays?"

Giles laughed warmly, though Gerard could argue in his head that the "warmth" made the hairs on his arm stand on end. "I'll admit I looked a little rough around the edges before." Running his fingers across the closely shaven side of his head, he pretended to be self-conscious. "What, is it too much?"

She smiled without teeth. If Giles chilled Gerard, he now knew who he'd learned the frigidity from. "No. It suits you perfectly."

The Speares ordered for their respective partners, pronouncing the French impeccably. "Do you want escargots?"

"Oh, I don't know. Gerard, how does escargots sound to you?"

"Mano, would you like escargots?"

The two men, stunned by this simultaneous attack, looked at each other for a cue, jaws ajar. The red in Gerard's face and ears augmented, and Mano looked as though he was going to die of mortification as the waiter stared at them both expectantly.

"Uh—yeah—"

"Escargots, that sounds—"

"Good," they finished together, but nodded dumbly like bobble heads.

After the waiter left to put in their orders, Gerard excused himself to go to the bathroom, figuring Mano was man enough to hold down the fort at the table. He stood in front of the mirror massaging his jaw, which seemed perfectly content hanging stupidly open. Tonight was, in Gerard's fantasies, supposed to be a night in which he felt okay assisting Mara in her familial self-destruction. Giles's appearance made everything so, so much worse.

"Du–ude, I can't believe what's going on over there." Mano entered the bathroom, giggling nervously like a boy.

Gerard's heart jumped at the Giles's date's presence. His mouth opened and closed, but he couldn't fathom the other man's foolishness. "You idiot," he hissed lowly, "why did you leave the two of them alone!? They're going to rip each other apart!"

Mano looked offended until he realized the gravity of the situation. "Oh shit, really?"

"No shit, really. I'm not Giles's father, if you haven't noticed."

"I know that, but, man, I know nothing about Giles's personal life," insisted Mano, as if that would fix everything. "We just fuck and watch movies!"

Gerard slapped his hand to his forehead. "I don't care what you guys do but—okay. We need to go back out there. Now."

He looked as though he would rather die than return to the passive-aggressive table. "No way, man, I'm ditching." Mano seemed to jump at the conveniently placed large window, but Gerard seized his arm.

"There is no way you're leaving me alone with them. We are going back out there."

Upon their return they discovered that, no, the two Speares had not ripped each other apart. In fact, they were laughing over the escargots. The air around Giles eased and Mara's closed-mouth smile relaxed in return. Gerard and Mano had had no reason to panic in the bathroom after all, as the dinner proceeded with much less tension. Mara continued on her bizarrely flirtatious path, which Gerard would have enjoyed had her son not been present. Everyone shared in the amusement of Mano struggling to pry the snail from its shell.

The four parted ways at the subway; Mano and Giles probably scurried off to a bar or to a movie. Despite Gerard's wishes to remain out while the night was young, Mara insisted they return to the Complexes before James came home for the night. Hand in his, she walked at a pace faster than Gerard was accustomed to. From behind, with her hair up and loose, she did, truly, look young as ever.

They escaped the cold, now biting, into the elevator, which was only slightly warmer. There, Mara threw her arms around Gerard's neck. With intense dark eyes and strange purposefulness, she repeated, "Do you love me, Gerard?"

All he could think about was the warmth of her ungloved hands on the back of his neck, the press of her body against his, and her warm breath palpably reaching up and embracing his face. "I love you, Mara."

The elevator creaked as they kissed. When the doors opened, Mara, laughing, rushed into E01, leaving him with a wave good-bye and a bizarre feeling that everything had gone wrong.

The walls were blue, the kind of blue that tended to remind Jessie of the sky. She couldn't help but think that they painted them blue to give their patients a false feeling of freedom. But, then again, she had to remind herself that "they" weren't the enemy here. If anything, she and her own impulsivity could be branded as the bad guy.

Again, she reprimanded herself for something that they called "black-and-white thinking." She wasn't very good at using the wise mind they promoted here; she was far too emotional, or far too emotionally rational, skewering the statistics to aid her depressive cause. There were a lot of things that she really ought to stop doing.

Despite the blue walls, the oppressive-like regimes, and the half-eager,

COMPLEXES

half-tired therapists, there was always something comforting about the hospital. Being shut out from the outside has its benefits, including clarity of mind. Here, in the hospital, was where she realized that Angus and Antony's argument probably had nothing to do with her. She also combated the thoughts of worthlessness and hopelessness with the excitement of going home again, to the Complexes. As much as she hated being home, stifled by cold, thin walls, where else was she to yearn for while trapped in inpatient? She missed her parents, cereal with marshmallows, and the freedom to not make your bed every morning. The wish to escape the hospital transcended her wish to die and was confused with a wish to live. So often was it in such institutions.

It was on her third day when her mother visited with a ripped piece of college ruled paper, bearing Angus's number on it. It was on her fourth when she finally resolved to call him. Telling people about her depression usually was an easy task for her—most of her friends knew and thus treaded lightly around her. But telling Angus felt different; it was like being diagnosed all over again. How would she even say it?

She scrambled to get her vitals checked and ate breakfast quickly to get to the phone first. Jessie waited for the little beep on the other line and immediately delved into her story. "I don't know if my mother told you already ... but I tried to kill myself the other day and now I'm in the hospital for inpatient care."

A short silence followed during which Jessie was unsure Angus was listening. Finally, he said, "I had no idea, Jess. I'm so sorry." His voice was low, as close to a whisper as a telephone would allow. "I wish I knew, somehow. I'm here for you, Jessie."

"It's okay, it's okay, don't apologize," she said, moving the phone from one ear to the other to keep her anxiety occupied. "It's just—I lost so many friends this past year and I almost thought I was going to lose you and Antony. And, I don't know, it's not just that, it's also that summer gets under my skin, you know? I feel unoccupied and distressed and ... all I'm saying is that it's not your fault."

"I don't know why you're on the phone trying to console me," Angus responded earnestly, "because I gave you my number so I could talk about you. Like, what you need and what can be done to help make things okay."

"Wow. Thanks," Jessie said, shocked at his maturity. Normally, people tended to make her problems their own, to swallow her up in some messed-up all-for-one-and-one-for-all treatment. Jessie hated that mentality, that enmeshing of feelings toward the point of suffocation. She hated that romantic dependence shown on television shows and depicted in young adult books. It was her ruin before; it would never be again. "You don't have to do anything, though. What happened between you and Antony is between you guys. Just ... I appreciate you being here for me, and I'd like it if we stayed friends."

Angus laughed heartily. The sound was like the whir of a heater on a cold day. It sounded strange, yet she was grateful. "Of course we'll stay friends," he said.

"How are the Complexes, by the way?" Jessie asked, glad to take a break from profundity. "And how are you?"

"The Complexes are still cold as ever."

"We have heating here."

"Goddamnit, you lucky girl."

Jessie smiled genuinely, for perhaps the first time in days. "I am a lucky girl," she mused aloud. "But you avoided my other question. How are you?"

A pause followed the parade of discourse. She knew Angus's personal life was a subject of great anxiety to him. Though she regretted pushing his buttons, her curiosity often got the better of her. If he just talked about it to someone, maybe he'd feel better about it, she figured.

"I'm good."

"That's good," Jessie replied nervously, knowing he dodged her purposefully.

CHAPTER SIX

Another silence ensued. She bit her lip, ripping off the membrane with her teeth. "I'm not that great, actually," Angus admitted. "But I think my family problems are the last thing you should be concerned about."

Jessie couldn't help but smile at his gentle consideration. "If you need to talk, I'm always here for you," she said, feeling the impact of her words in her own chest. "I need to focus on myself right now but ... when I get out, I'm all ears. I promise."

"It's a hell of a story," Angus warned, half jokingly. "But I think some outside feedback would help, yeah."

"Yeah." Her grin was as wide as the Pacific. "They're yelling at me to get off the phone now, but I'll call you back some other time. Talk to you later?"

"Later, then."

She hung up and attended group therapy, fully determined to leave the hospital on a resounding high note

COMPLEXES

Chapter Seven

On his first outing without Giles in half a year, Jonathan felt stared at, naked, and exploited, like a piece of paper topped with dried glue. He maneuvered his way through this frat house party expecting very little except to get very drunk.

"Where's your boyfriend?" a classmate casually asked just when Jonathan was getting buzzed. He begrudgingly explained that, no, Giles wasn't his boyfriend. Though, he couldn't quite find an answer to the "where" part of her question. That was a figurative punch to the gut.

A couple of drinks later and further drunken crowd jostling led him to a quieter corner of the party, where a couple of students blockaded the bedroom from horny couples in need of privacy. "It's funny to see how desperate they get to get in each other's pants," one young man, vaguely familiar to Jonathan, explained with a laugh. "Will they fuck each other on the washing machine? Or in the shadow of the house?"

Half wishing to fall asleep, Jonathan settled on the bed and watched this small, tight-knit group interact. "We're all philosophy majors, in some form or another," explained the girl sitting beside him, cross-legged like Giles. "Frat parties are okay, but we always end up someplace quiet. Don't we, Xavier?"

The man who seemed the life of the group, who'd explained their blockade earlier, turned his head and laughed again. "I'm a photography major, don't bunch me up with you guys," he said to the girl, who conceded gently. "And the redhead is?"

"A fine arts major," he piped in. "The name's Jonathan."

"Jo–onathan," Xavier exclaimed with a swig of his drink. He ungracefully plopped himself beside Jonathan and put his arm around him. "Here's to creators, foraging their way forward instead of dwelling in the past."

The girl beside them grimaced. "Philosophy majors don't 'dwell,' " she argued.

"Hey, hey, hey, all to one's own. But we creators gotta stick together, eh, Jonathan?"

And so the night continued, Xavier talking at Jonathan with his arm wrapped around him, and Jonathan mostly listening to the slight murmur of what must be profound philosophic conversation about the meaning of life. "I want to leave this place," Xavier said, somehow finding himself explaining his life dreams to a stranger. "It's gonna get too cold, and then it's going to snow, and then it's going to freeze. Let's go somewhere temperate. Like Italy."

COMPLEXES

Jonathan, getting sleepy, rested his head on Xavier's shoulder. "Italy sounds lovely," he mumbled, thinking of Giles and how lovely his lanky body was.

He thought of Giles when he kissed Xavier Eslava, and he pushed Giles away when Xavier kissed him back. The philosophy majors, bent on maintaining platonic peace, kicked the two out of their bedroom abode. "I guess we're the desperate ones now," Xavier said, laughing.

Putting on their best sober faces, they took a taxi to the Complexes. Xavier's arm was still warm around Jonathan. The crevice between Xavier's shoulder and neck felt safe. They took the elevator up, appreciating the slow lift. Jonathan struggled with the keys to E07, and when he managed to turn the doorknob, he and Xavier tumbled in like excited children.

"Who the hell are you?"

Jonathan had figured that Giles was with Mano. He had figured wrong.

Xavier giggled drunkenly, looking from Giles to Jonathan and back. "You didn't tell me you had a roommate," he said, still sporting an amused grin.

Cursing his luck, Jonathan slapped on the most serious face he could muster. "I didn't think my 'roommate' was around."

"Sorry, but it looks like you have to go home." Giles crossed his arms, looking as defiant as Gandalf when he said "You shall

207

not pass!" "Where do you live? I'll walk you to a taxi."

Xavier agreed to leave, much to Jonathan's dismay. "Sorry, man," he said. "We'll meet another time? I live in the Complexes, floor G. Or ... is that floor seven? Ha-ha. I don't know."

"We are in the Complexes, you drunken dolt." Giles shook his head and guided Xavier out. In the meantime, Jonathan kicked the leg of the bed, wondering when Giles had gotten home and when Giles had begun dictating what he did with his life. A few minutes later, when Giles returned into E07, Jonathan had no qualms about yelling multiple vulgarities in his general direction.

He wasn't amused. "Are you done? Here, have some water." Defiant Jonathan refused to imbibe anything that wasn't beer, but when Giles passed him the water and guided the cup to his mouth, he happily drank. Afterward, he found himself in between bedsheets and blankets, comfortably tucked in like a child. All along, he mumbled, "Fuck you, Giles ... fuck you."

Giles stroked his curly hair, thinking nothing of Jonathan's incoherent cursing. "Whatever you say, Nathan," he said lowly, lulling him to sleep. "Whatever you say."

❄ ❄ ❄ ❄ ❄

Twenty dollars was a small price to pay for passport photos. A mutual friend referred her to a certain young Mr. Eslava, who had turned his floor G apartment room into a fancy photography shindig. Roonie winced at the bright lights; Xavier Eslava asked as the photo was taken, "Where are you going?"

"I don't know yet," she admitted. The camera clicked again. She strained her eyes to keep them from blinking. "Do you have any suggestions?"

Eslava, noticeably curious, printed out her photos and gave them to her for inspection. "Well—I was thinking Italy at first. But then, I thought—nah, that's too typical of an escape hatch. So maybe, someplace cooler—I mean, hotter. I saw this CNN expose on the food in Thailand, and thought, yeah, it would be awesome to go there."

Roonie considered it: a young Latino college student and an ex-whore African-American, off in a journey through Thailand? It took her a second to realize she was overstepping herself—Xavier was a stranger, not even an acquaintance on Facebook. "Thailand," she mused aloud. "I'd be too afraid to go alone."

"It was just a suggestion." He laughed.

But by the end of the night, after giving Roonie a crash course in photography, Xavier had his own passport photos printed out. "This is the craziest thing I've ever done," he admitted after they booked the flight and accidentally printed out the confirmation email on Xavier's photo paper. Roonie nearly agreed; but "crazy" was relative, wasn't it?

She once thought it was crazy to give blow jobs in return for hard cash. It might have perturbed her the first few times, but the nagging sensation of immorality was buried under some false independence and strange feminism. "I can suck dicks for money if I want to," she challenged a friend who protested against her behavior. "Stop stigmatizing sex and women." Besides, the money usually went straight to her tuition—both parties were happy, no harm done.

But the bases soon were overrun, and college was only a temporary excuse. Roonie found herself floating in the semi-unsatisfied paste of life. The degree, as compared to her new profession, was useless to her. She didn't want to go. But if she did, she couldn't.

Roonie never explained how trapped she felt to anyone. Thus, she couldn't fathom why Sans gave what he gave—how he could have known of her unspoken plight. Did the look on her face in the hallways give it away? Did her footsteps sound hollow?

Now when she walked the halls of the Complexes, she always gave a glance, something like an affirmative nod, to the cameras. "I'm doing it," she hoped her body language said. "I'm taking your money, and I'm going away." Perhaps she was trying to convince herself more than anything.

COMPLEXES

Was she running away from her problems? Roonie figured, with a lot of dedication, she could just as easily find a job in the city as a waitress while writing freelance for magazines and newspapers. Eventually luck would turn her way. She didn't need someone's charity.

What she did need, however, was a push into the deep end to learn to tread. That suitcase full of money violently shoved her into the depths of Asia.

Thailand. They have wonderful food, according to that one CNN special. They say it's warmer there. They say there's hope yet.

As Roonie looked out the window, flurries tumbled, swinging side to side in midair before merging with the damp concrete. The city slept early, woke up late, and stayed in bed, without the energy to even properly wash its face. The jagged teeth of the cityscape merged with the grayness of the sky.

There may be hope in Thailand, but there is no hope left here.

Varying levels of panic permeated through the grocery stores; Antony unwillingly contributed to it as he stocked his bags with loads of microwavable breakfast burritos, cup ramen, and all the other healthier foods that Ruthy demanded he purchase. Antony checked out and trudged his way toward the Complexes, secretly enjoying the sound of his boots squishing the snow.

Once he reached the building and waved a brief hello to Sans, he entered the elevator and waited rather impatiently for the doors to close.

"Hold it!"

Just barely barring the door from closing with his arm, Antony looked up to see who he had just aided. He, brown haired and burly, was James Speare. He only gave Antony a slightly bizarre and pained look. Gulping back his fear and forbidden knowledge, Antony mumbled a faint "You're welcome" as a response to the nonexistent thank-you.

The elevator squealed in protest as it moved up. Antony leaned against the wall with a vain hand on his ear. James stood like an oak tree in the center of the enclosed space, looking straight before him, looking as if he were mumbling to himself. Once the doors opened, revealing floor E, Antony darted out so quickly that he forgot one bag of groceries on the elevator floor. Only realizing this halfway toward his apartment, he turned around, face flaming red from embarrassment. James had picked up the plastic bag and held it out toward him. When Antony grasped the handles to take it, he found that James wasn't going to let go.

James said, more harsh than concerned, "Where's your mother, boy?"

212

COMPLEXES

"Gone." Antony pulled away with the bag and said nothing else. He scurried into E11 and shut the door resoundingly, hoping the door would speak for his rage. Who the hell spews out things like that? "Where's your mother, boy?" Antony mimicked hatefully as he put the groceries away.

She was easy to forget as long as no one brought her up. As much as he liked to pretend it didn't bother him that she was gone, it often times did. It sure as hell bothered his father, who was currently in the love throes in search of the past, a past that Antony never fucking shared. When Gerard came home from work complaining that he couldn't return if the snow didn't end, Antony was tempted to curse and yell at him and ask him where his mother went. *The husband of the woman you're with asked me very rudely where my mother was. I didn't even have an accurate answer. Do you know how much that hurts?*

His silence was telling. He didn't really want to know, did he? He didn't want to know the sob story that ruined his father's psyche. He didn't want to know that she was either dead or full of hate.

Then, he thought of Morrissey and her own slice of the ignorance pie, and buried his face in the dark embrace of comforter and pillows, and remained there until a howl of wind woke him up.

CHAPTER SEVEN

She wondered if he could count her stretch marks, or if he noticed how her left breast sagged a little lower than the right one, all because Angus preferred to suck on it more for milk when he was a baby. Her jeans fit a little looser than last week, and she felt self-conscious about her eyes. Still, when she looked at Gerard, she knew she was loved. With a forced smile she advanced, kissing him until she cried.

"I'm going to leave your father," she had told Giles that other night at the Relais d'Auvergne. "I found a man who loves me for who I am. And I'm going to leave."

Giles closed his eyes, as if somewhere inside him the answer was buried. He settled on, "If it's best."

"You left first," Mara criticized.

"Do you ever wonder," he cut in, twirling his finger on the rim of his wineglass, "why we're in this city rather than home? No, I didn't leave first, Mom. Father did."

Her back might have straightened, but she emotionally deflated. Broken, she said, "Then what's wrong with me leaving if everyone else is gone?"

"Nothing is." Giles shook his head, wearing a pained smile. "I just wish it was different."

But it wasn't different, and Mara couldn't waste her time musing, home alone, on the what-ifs. She felt young, hell,

214

she was young, and now that the snow was falling in earnest she wanted to snatch everything that ever meant anything to her and run before it was too late. Angus would be furious, but she could take him with her. And Giles could handle himself on his own. Fuck James.

And at the thought of her husband, at the sensation of Gerard's hand on her left breast, she collapsed and wept.

Gerard's mouth opened and closed, grabbing at remnants of words but finding nothing much to say. "Did I do something wrong?" he asked. Mara didn't—or rather, failed to—respond. How could she explain, after so much commitment, after beginning her dig into a new hopeless tunnel, that she had changed her mind? She was lonely, yes, but Gerard wasn't the man she wanted, ideal and dashing and polite as he was. "Mara," Gerard began to speak, but she hated the sound of her name intimate on his tongue.

It was all wrong, and she had no idea how to fix it. After bandages and stitches and transfusions and splints and tourniquets and amputation, the infection, the goddamn tumor or whatever the hell it was, still remained as a plague on her house.

"I have to—I have to go," Mara stammered, inching away from Gerard, afraid to feel his skin against hers. She refused to see his heartbroken expression, knowing it would be the end of her. She snatched her shirt and with shaky hands put it on and darted out the door.

"Wait! Wait—" Gerard's voice might as well have come from a kicked dog. Her heart pounded in agony for him. She'd used him. And now she was leaving him, too.

Her hands quavered at the doorknob to E01. The keys refused to remain steady, and they fell like heavy weights to the floor twice. "Please, open up." She weakly knocked, unsure, even at the late hour, if anyone was home. Resting her wet cheek on the door, she slammed it with the palm of her hand, in sheer frustration. In any moment, she could turn back and apologize to Gerard and sleep with him like she planned. This door hovered in her mind, symbolic of the words she refused to say and the steps she was too frightened to take. Behind it, every ounce of joy she left in Italy, every pound she pushed out in childbirth, and every seam of clothing she sewed in Calcutta.

The door opened, and Mara tumbled, like a twittering bird learning to fly again, into James's arms.

He was quiet, and yet she continued to roar with emotion. Her tongue stumbled on her teeth until the words burst from her, like blood from her own wounds, "Do you love me, James?"

His face hardened. His eyebrows became thick wrinkles that seemed to consume him. Terrified, Mara almost looked away.

"I do love you, Mara. You have to believe me," he murmured, forehead against hers. "I thought you stopped loving me long ago."

"After all these years?"

"I never knew how to do this, the life of a husband, the life of a father. After a while, I thought you were using me. And when I pushed you away, I wanted you to come back, but you never did. And you looked as though you didn't care. I know my face doesn't say it right, and my actions were far from what you want, but you have to believe me. I love you. I love you."

Her final tears slipped from her eyes. Mara laughed, in utter disbelief, stupefied by the Dickensian outcome, how complicated a simple thing called communication seemed, and how maybe, just maybe, resolution was possible, closer by an eyelash's breadth, even when it was so close in the first place.

The cold, almost a refreshing change of pace from the warmth of a radiator, cast a spell worthy of all the ice queens in literature combined. Marie drove like a skidding snail to bring her home, and yet Jessie kept her window down the entire drive, allowing the flakes to tumble into the car and into her slightly open mouth. When her mother protested to the cold and waste of battery-generated heat, Jessie only shot her a dark look and continued to swallow the flakes.

Her room never looked so comfortable. Jessie always slept with an overwhelming amount of pillows; the unfluffed single pillow at the hospital left her wanting home more than she could ever imagine. She could have her own bathroom again. She could wear earrings again. She could talk about potentially harmful things without someone calling them "maladaptive coping skills" again.

In light of this, her recovery felt like a wasteful scam. They shove you in a place you don't want to be, dangling freedom tied with the idea of recovery, and expect you to never come back. Jessie despondently realized she'd learned nothing in the hospital, other than how to pretend to look okay.

The conversation with Angus was nice, though.

Oh, Angus. She had to tell him she was home. As much as it pained her to part from her welcoming bed, she left her room and exited to the hallway, which, she found, was considerably colder than her room. The slap of frigid air, deceptively fresh as a breath mint, had Jessie wishing she could sleep for another year or so, until this godless world regained its heat, or at least until her life started again.

She was waiting, as always. This thought wrenched her chest and pushed her heart against her rib cage. What was she waiting for? A new opportunity, a new muse, perhaps, would distract her, but then she'd retreat back into her depressive shelter once the bombs started falling again. Another suicide attempt, to Jessie, was inevitable. Another cut, another day.

"Do you need help?" A woman, dark skinned and tall, cut through her reverie.

It took a visible moment for the woman's presence to settle into her head. When she took in her appearance, she remembered her from that day when Sans threw the stress ball at Antony. "Oh," she said. "No, I'm just … thinking. Thank you, though." Jessie shrugged her shoulders and contemplated reentering her room. Before the woman, Roonie, could turn around and walk away, Jessie asked, "Actually—um, is it true?"

Roonie paused deliberately, as if she knew what was coming. "Is what true?"

"That you're …" *As self-hating as I am?*

"Is it true that you tried to kill yourself twice?" she cut in, voice sounding as harsh as the concrete but expression as soft as the snow covering it.

Jessie sighed, unhurt, but still defeated. "Touché. I think that lately I've been going insane. Asking too many piercing questions, to myself and to others. I figure third time's the charm, so I might as well get everything out of the way now."

"Third time's the charm?" Roonie looked at her incredulously, eyes a dark mirror into Jessie's world. Hearing the words on another person's tongue, Jessie's hand flew up to her mouth, palm slapping against her lips, and tears the only warm thing in the hallway.

Then, open arms pulled Jessie in, cold skin and wretched heart and all. "Someday," Roonie told her, "you will be saved. You will hate every moment of it; you will hate every inch of the face of your savior. But once you're out of that dark place, you will look at that person and see it was you all along."

Roonie released her, patted her on her fuzzed head, and turned around, evidently not expecting a thank-you. Even if she asked for one, Jessie wouldn't be ready for proper gratitude. Roonie had told her something invaluable, something that she herself hadn't quite applied to her own life, but was trying to. She left Jessie to mull over her life, pick and choose death as if it were an optional topping on a burrito.

And Jessie knew it was true, she knew she had to save herself, but goddamnit, it was so hard.

COMPLEXES

Chapter Eight

When Angus woke up—for sleeping was the only thing to do when it was snowing out—he found his parents, quiet, at the dinner table, one hand in the other's. Mara was in tears—despite it being nothing new, she always tore at his wounded heart with her salted tears. "Angus," she said, noticing his entrance, "come, sit down." Fight-or-flight instincts raised the hairs on his arms and neck. When he looked to his father, he saw the same expressionless mug he stared at and tried to impress and tried to change in his dreams with surgical scalpels. "Please?" Mara asked, wiping her tears away brusquely with her thumb, as if she were prepared to drop an atomic bomb on Japan. At that, Angus couldn't say no.

"What's going on?" he said, feeling the awkward hardness of the chair on his back and bottom. Again, he looked to his father for some sort of cue or clue, and received nothing but blankness. Angus's fists tightened at the very sight.

"Your father and I—we have decided that we need to talk." In moments like these, Angus could tell that English wasn't his mother's first language. She spoke like the words were harder to say than they really were, hard as marbles overflowing in her mouth.

CHAPTER EIGHT

Looking squarely at his father, Angus chanced a guess. "Are you getting a divorce?"

An open palm slammed on the table. "Damn it, Angus!" was all that his father could manage. His face looked strained, pained, and every word that rhymed and fit the aesthetic of "trying but unable to." With his mother's arm gently touching his, he sat back down and cleared his throat. Much more calmly, but still with that ridiculous expression, he managed, "We're not getting a divorce. We're going to try."

"Try?" Angus snorted, purposefully pushing their buttons to hear what he wanted to hear. "Try for what? A regular, ordinary family that actually talks to each other? Or—or maybe, even though you're both too old, another baby that you can fuck up like you did me and Giles?"

The temporary dam in his mother's eyes didn't work for long. She blinked, and her tears spilled over her eroded cheeks, "Angus, no," she said in something that sounded pitifully like a whimper. "We really want to be a family."

Angus's jaw felt heavy and strong. Well, here they were, talking, like he always wanted them to. He clutched the sides of his chair, and, feeling like his guts were spilling from his stomach, said, "You don't try to be a family. You are a family or you're not. And a good way to start is to—to—to tell each other that you love each other—and to—to not be afraid of each other—and to not kick each other out—and to accept and kiss each other even though we might wince away and—" Slapping a hand on his mouth, Angus rested his forehead on the table, feeling the heaving breaths and the long-gone tears spring up to dampen the dry leaves that colored his eyes.

A hand rested on his shoulder, far too large to be his mother's. Angus sat up and felt arms embrace him, tightly, hands grasping the extra skin on the back of his neck. His father said nothing else. And suddenly, Angus felt like a child again, looking up and seeing nothing but an ear and a shoulder, but knowing that if he dared look to the side he'd see his father, smiling and proud.

"We're starting now, Angus," his mom said, reaching over and occupying Angus's free hand with hers. "And I promise, and your father promises, too, we're going to talk and tell each other things and do everything you said you wanted us to do. Because that's what a family does."

Angus's dad released him, with a smile—albeit a bit grim one—on his face. "Why don't you ever look happy?" Angus asked him, face still contorted by his own emotions. "When I was a child, I guess you looked happy, but as I grew up, it was as if everything glad about you was sucked out with age." Afraid to see his father, he looked away. "I remember your face when I was little, but now that I'm older—am I a different person than you expected? Is there something wrong with me that you always look so sour?"

Once again, his father grimaced at his son's words, and struggled to find his own. "I don't know what to do, sometimes," he admitted, the sadness hinted through his voice, "but never for one moment was I not proud of you."

Angus chewed on his lip, and, although unsure, he conceded. "Okay … Dad." He looked up at the table, at his family, and still sensed a noticeable emptiness within them. "Giles, what about Giles?" He looked hopefully at his father, who seemed a tad incensed at the very name but remained silent.

"We're going to talk to him," his mom said. "I said we're going to be a family—that means all of us. Isn't that right, James?" With another disturbed expression, he agreed with a nod. After Angus insisted that they be gentle on Giles, the winds shook at the windows—the peaceful snow had transformed into a blizzard. He got up from his chair and peered outside at the snow, compiling slowly like the pages of a novel. His mother followed behind him, and eventually came to his side and rested her hand on his head. The family, becoming three-fourths complete as his father joined them, faced a future not as bleak as the past.

COMPLEXES

The panic settled in like food dye in milk. Gerard took a swig of his booze, counting down his dollars so quickly that he wouldn't have noticed his fingers trembling like the ends of delicate branches. It was time to regroup, replant, and ease his roots elsewhere. Ignoring the howling of the storm, he went into his rooms and packed his boxes and bags as tightly as possible. He planned on leaving as many empty shells behind as possible, coy reminders of his presence.

Gerard had made a mistake. Understandable, it was. He had given in to lust and what he thought was love. What else was he supposed to think when multiple arms and words and tongues drew him in, tugging him toward her naked torso? She consented, and he told her that he loved her—what else was missing?

Ah. It wasn't mutual. She was fucking using him to massage the worries out of her brains with little kisses and a touch of tongue. And now that she was done with him, wiped him off and threw him out like the hard shell of an avocado, she was more than gone. She was never to return, too ashamed of her mistake to look back at the discarded skin, the ravaged man who only wanted her love. *Oops. Be a darling and clean up my mess, will you?*

Yeah, he was cleaning up, all right, straight out of the state. And he'd be damned before he allowed himself to be caught weak by another woman. Next time he'd find the one and sweep her off her feet and make sure that she loved him as much as he loved her—if only it were that easy. In his panic, he forgot the sensation, the trickling down of love, of when he first met Mara. Was it love? He couldn't tell anymore. Before and after Alice, he couldn't tell anymore.

Loudly the packaging tape screeched as he sealed another filled box. He cursed as his thumb ran against the teeth of the tape dispenser. Blood needlessly dripped from his finger. What a waste of blood. What a waste of feeling!

Mara was a waste, this stop at the city was a waste, and they had to get out—*now*—

"Dad."

Antony opened the door, having trudged through inches of snow for the milk that Gerard forgot he asked for. His eyes widened at the sight of the room, already half tucked away for a trip elsewhere. The hallway light behind him seemed too bright for Gerard. Squinting up at his son, Gerard stood, and took him by the shoulders. "We're leaving. Now."

"What?" Antony half laughed, half hissed. It was a horrible sound, as if he expected this very encounter and was snorting at the irony. "Where?"

"We've got enough money for a flight. Let's go ... San Diego. Or—or San Francisco. Where you were born. You'd like that, wouldn't you?"

COMPLEXES

With intense, overexaggerated movements, as if he were a comedian behind a microphone stand, Antony placed the milk on the table, rubbed his chin in thought, and finally said, "Yes, I would like that, but I don't really want that. You feel me?"

Gerard, exasperated by his son's silly behavior, said as menacingly as he could manage, "I'm not joking, Antony. Get to your room and start packing." He turned his back and continued to place his wide array of plain T-shirts into a duffel bag.

One word, defiant, challenged Gerard's emotions to no end. "No," Antony said, as if what Gerard had suggested was the most inhumane, disgusting thing.

Straightening his back, knowing he could look as intimidating as James if he tried, Gerard faced his son. He hadn't realized that they were squarely eye-to-eye. It was like he was looking through a time portal—except Antony had his mother's softness. Disregarding that, he faced him down just as he faced himself down minutes before. "I made a mistake coming here. And we're going to do this just as we do everything."

Antony grimaced and blurted, tongue hanging out stupidly, "Together?"

"This is not a joke."

Face back to normal, Antony retorted, in a slightly more serious manner, "Yeah, but I'm sick of following your rules,

CHAPTER EIGHT

Dad. For one, you said it yourself, Ruthy needs us. For two, hell if I'm leaving Morrissey to care for her sick mother. Oh, and let's not forget the giant fucking blizzard outside."

Gerard scowled. "That stuff hasn't stopped us before. Quit whining." He threw his son a shirt that lay haphazardly on the sofa. "We're going."

Catching the shirt only to throw it back childishly, he said, "I'm afraid your age is making you hard of hearing. No means no, Dad, if you haven't checked the consent commercials. Mara told you no, and I'm telling you no, so let's stay here and watch the snow because, yet again, we have failed to buy a television as our monthly investment. Agreed?"

Tossing the shirt to the ground, Gerard felt a growl push from his veins through his throat and into the air. "Goddamnit, son, I'm going to drag you onto that plane even if it's by the tiny hairs on your scalp."

Antony, only amused by the dirt underneath his fingernails, simply replied, "Go without me, then. I'm not stopping you."

"Why do you want to stay so badly?" Despite his knowing that the wrathful route had failed, Gerard couldn't help but feel absolutely furious at his son's random defiance. Years have passed, and sure, Antony at times protested, but not like this. The one second during which Gerard

228

entertained the thought of travelling on his own hurt him more than Mara's rejection.

"Dad, if you haven't noticed: it's not getting any warmer. According to the radio this blizzard will go on for weeks." Antony crossed his arms and shrugged his shoulders, attempting to look nonchalant about his next words. "I don't want to live running away and searching anymore. And more than that, I don't want to die someplace cold and unfamiliar."

With that, Gerard's half-drunken rage was over. With eyes brimmed, he clutched onto Antony's sleeve. He was, after all, his final lifeline. Still half-furious but mostly dripping with fear, he said, "Don't you go talking about dying on me, son. Not on my watch."

Taking his father's paled hand, Antony concluded, "We're staying."

Thus, the Shepherds remained in the Complexes. Gerard's dreams catching skirts ended. Perhaps he stopped dreaming altogether. There was a numbness in his heart that pumped even colder blood through his veins. But his son was there, and, like sunshine in snow, he could still smile and point to Antony and say that he hadn't quite failed. No, no matter how many times he fucked up, he hadn't failed at all.

CHAPTER EIGHT

"What a surprise, Mr. Speare! No Mr. Gillian today? That's all right, that's all right. I have two guests already with me, if you don't mind the extra company." Martha shut the door behind Giles and shuffled her way to the tea table, which, much to Giles's shock and disbelief, was occupied by James and Mara Speare. His comfort zone totally encroached, he was tempted to exit the building and enter the searing cold to cool his heated emotions. There was, however, a game to play—Giles could tell by the solemn look eternally plastered on his father's face. So he politely helped Martha prepare the tea—oolong, for today—and sat while the kettle warmed up.

Martha tittered comfortably, clearly unaware of the tension in the room. "Where is Mr. Gillian? I hardly see you two apart, it's like you're twins!"

Giles laughed warmly at the idea; he and Jonathan were, truly, far from twins. "We're more like ..." he began, then stopped himself after becoming abruptly aware of his father's stern presence. Then again, what stopped him before? "Lovers," he finished, somewhat wistfully. Lovers. Perhaps in an alternate universe with an alternate Giles, they would be. In this sad reality, he and Jonathan hadn't properly spoken for a while. They let the DVDs speak for themselves, and fell asleep close, but not close enough to feel each other's warmth.

The distance was frightening, but it was what was comfortable for Giles.

COMPLEXES

Mara stuttered her way into the boiling conversation. She declared meekly, "We would like you back in our home, Giles."

He had considered that. But what would it accomplish? More false statements of how the family would stumble through life somehow intact? He didn't want that. To be earnest, he didn't want anything breakable—which was, probably, why he was alone. The kettle screeched, and Giles got up to pour the tea, focusing hard to keep his hands from shaking. After all this time, his calm façade was breaking.

"Oolong tea?" Martha commented critically after taking a daring sip at the scalding drink. "I never liked oolong tea. It reminds me of those cheap Chinese restaurants downtown with all the dead flies in the gutter."

"They may be cheap," Giles replied, "but they are authentic. And the food is delicious. Isn't that right, Mother?" He smiled, as sincerely as his face could manage, at Mara, who looked simply shocked at her son's audacity. Once again she stammered, glancing desperately at James to say something. Naturally, he remained quiet.

Mara temporarily regained her voice only to weakly assert, "Please don't ignore us. We want you home. Angus wants you home. James wants you home."

CHAPTER EIGHT

At the practiced repetition, something seemed to click in Martha. "You know, I've lived in the Complexes all my life. And I never understood why it gets so cold in here! My bones are frigid! Maybe I really am getting old." She turned her head and gazed out the window meaningfully. "It's August. I don't remember it snowing in August before. That's curious."

Giles gently placed his hand on hers, insisting kindly, "You're not getting old, Martha. Winter just came early this year."

"Stop playing games, Giles, please," Mara pleaded, her eyes narrowing to dam up the tears. "Don't tell her lies, Giles. And don't you dare ignore us."

Her words sparked a furious fire in Giles. He arched an eyebrow and challenged, "Us?" He gestured to James and Mara, and repeated in a wondering tone, "You're an 'us' now?"

James's low voice seemed to come from the deep itself. "Don't be rude to your mother."

Unafraid, Giles continued to press their exposed buttons. "Oh, I'm sorry, was I being rude? I didn't mean it." He beamed at them, the sarcasm overflowing like honey from his mouth.

"Giles, we're not playing around. We already talked, as a family, and we want to start over again."

"You sound ridiculous, Father. We already talked? As a family? Start over again? What in hell has possessed you to think that talking a little bit is going to fix everything? Do you know that he cheated on you, Mother? Do you know that he moved here to continue his affair with said woman? Have you ever wondered why he never showed an ounce of affection to his sons, to you, ever since this family began? Angus learned his anger from someone. And I just happened to learn my 'games' from you, silent Mother-dear. So what do you want me to do? Come back and sing kum-ba-yah and pray that everything won't go to shit again? Fuck that. And fuck y—"

Martha, no matter how frail, slapped Giles good and hard, hard enough for the impact of skin on skin to be audible. A red spot slowly grew to glow on his skin. He breathed loudly, visibly astonished at what had just occurred, if not also the words that had come from his own mouth.

"Let's talk," Martha began, as if she were going to give a dignified lecture, "and have tea, like a gentleman, now, Mr. Speare. Go on, drink up." Giles stared at the old woman incredulously but obeyed her and drank the earthy oolong. "Now then. What were you saying about winter?"

"Winter ..." Giles murmured after her, aimlessly spitting out words to erase his shame. The windows strained against the wind outside. Snow piled up against the glass. It was cold in Martha's room, easily at freezing. "Don't you need a jacket, Martha?" Giles asked, hoping it would suffice as an apology. Martha was all too happy to comply and retrieve her jacket from her closet, leaving the Speares temporarily to their tea.

"Giles, I don't think you realize," Mara said, quietly, but with regained strength, "that talking is really what we have to do."

Putting a hand to his face, to the mark that Martha left on his cheek, he said, "I already know that, Mom." He looked at Martha's freshly vacated chair, and wondered when, if ever, had anyone timed such a movement with so much poise. After imagining a young woman with Rosie-the-Riveter-like spunk, Giles knew that simply was not her. Martha was old, but she had an arm, and she knew—she knew when to use it.

So he took a deep breath and wore his shame clearly on his cheek. With a tone as straightforward as possible, he began the conversation he ought to have started a year ago. "Why did you cheat on Mom?"

COMPLEXES

Chapter Nine

Antony shot off a text to Jessie and Angus, the first one in ages. "Urgent!" it read, "Meet me down at the boiler room ASAP." Gleefully, with poster board and a fading marker, he wrote once again his protest's terms and conditions on one side, and a blazing, *NO SLEEP 'TIL HEAT* on the other. He slid down the banisters via his bottom. It was a good day, he felt, and soon, it would become even better.

Jessie was the first to arrive, clad in a sweatshirt and her kangaroo pants and sporting newly buzzed hair. "Hey," she declared, hands tucked in her pockets. "Long time, no see, Antony." As a response, he flourished the sign and ran up a few steps to hug her. She smiled at him and asked, with a hint of anxiety in her voice, "Is Angus coming too?"

"Yup. We're going to protest our asses off."

They passed a few minutes sitting on the cold ground, mostly in silence. Antony nearly sent Angus a reminder text until the boy appeared at the staircase, perceptibly perplexed. "Aw, hell no," he cried aloud once he read the sign. "We are not doing this again."

Antony pouted. "Where's your sense of justice? My thermometer says it's below freezing. I don't know about yours, but I need heat, and I need heat now." He waved the sign in the air for emphasis and opened his mouth to scream his slogan until Jessie playfully punched him in the shoulder.

Angus grumbled, but he sat down next to Antony anyway. "Does Miriam even come down to the boiler room at this time?"

"Nope," Antony said. "But I slipped her a note. No sleep 'til heat!" Even though there was no one around them, Angus and Jessie buried their faces in their hands for fear of embarrassment. Antony chanted alone for a solid six minutes before resting his voice. "Whoo," he exhaled, "that was refreshing. Your turn, Angus."

Slowly, Angus explained as if to a stubborn child, "No one comes down here, and no one will hear you."

"Was I not loud enough? NO—" Jessie frantically covered Antony's mouth with her hands. He finally conceded, grinning, "Okay, okay, I'll shut up."

A long silence ensued—when Antony wasn't making noise, there wasn't any. Jessie shifted to a more comfortable position on the floor; Angus rested his head in his hands and could have appeared asleep. Unamused by their boredom, Antony barked a loud "Hey!" causing the two to wince at the sudden bang of voice. "Let's play a game while we wait," he suggested, eager as a child. "Truth or dare?"

"What are we, twelve?" Angus challenged, rolling his eyes.

COMPLEXES

Antony rearranged his words. "Truth for truth for truth, then."

Jessie crossed her legs, looking more attentive. "Okay," she surrendered. To Angus, who made an irked face, she said, "Just play along. We're here, anyway." He sighed a vague "fine" and Antony cackled evilly to exaggerate his victory.

"I start," Angus said.

Antony rejected the idea. "You want to start? You didn't even want to play!"

"I start or no game," he stated definitively. "Antony—the hell was your dad thinking when he had that fling with my mom?"

Jessie's eyes flickered between the two boys, her sleeved hand covering the inevitable nervous expression on her face. Sobered up by the question, Antony responded fairly, "I can't speak for my dad. But I know that he fell in love with your mom. And, for the record, she came onto him and asked him to go out with her." He paused, mulling over his words, only to reach a silly but strange conclusion: "Man, they're adults, but they sound just like teenagers."

Surprisingly, Angus accepted the answer with no grudges. He would be no more hostile to Antony than what was natural to him.

"Are we at peace?" Jessie asked, biting at a hangnail nervously. Noticing her apprehension, Antony wrapped his arm around her shoulder and nodded at Angus, who nodded back. Her spine, he felt, released some of its tautness. Huh, a few words and last month's problem wouldn't have occurred at all.

"My turn," Antony said, releasing Jessie from his hold only to take her by her shoulders. "Do you need help right now?" he asked her, looking intensely into her eyes.

Jessie considered this for a second, before providing him a confused, "No?"

"Okay. But whenever you do, you can always holler at me," he finished, releasing his grip on her and laughing as if saying such a thing was normal.

Jessie, slightly mortified, mumbled a faint thank-you. She fumbled with her hands in her sweatshirt, trying to think of a question to ask either of them. "Angus," she decided, "is my hair weird, or am I just overthinking things?"

After reaching over to touch the entirely buzzed head, Angus concluded, "You're just overthinking things." While they smiled at each other, fuzzed by perceptible feelings of romance, Antony made strange faces at them in the background. Not that he minded the fact that the two were probably going to go out in the near future—he simply figured, hey, might as well practice being the awkwardly unoiled third wheel.

Before Angus could conjure a question for his turn, Jessie delved into her confession. "Antony, I have something to say. I figure you ought to know, since we're stuck here and all. It's a big part of my life." Despite his already having figured it out, Antony patiently let her talk about her twenty-first-century rendition of the pursuit of happiness. After admitting that she had made an attempt on her life last month, the words flowed out of her as if she were telling a story that wasn't quite hers. "There's more to it …" Jessie hesitated, gauging the emotions of her audience, before finally saying, "But I think that's for another time."

"Can I hug you?" Antony asked, widening his arms to let her in. Gladly she hugged him, resting her chin on his shoulder. "Hey, you," Antony hissed at Angus, making vague facial gestures at him. "Get in here. She needs a good hug."

"Ugh, for real?" Angus groaned, but as usual, he submitted to Antony's wishes, not because of any sense of obligation, but because of a respect he had for these two. Antony could tell that, the more Angus complained, the more he cared. It was a silly method of expression, easily misconstrued, but Antony let him in anyway.

"This is cute. A hippie protest?"

The villain had arrived to ruin the hug. The three broke apart, two faces red and one face prepared to fight. "No sleep 'til heat!" battle-cried Antony, raising his makeshift sign in the air. Miriam raised her eyebrows and nodded her head, simply

CHAPTER NINE

amused by their shenanigans. "Seriously, woman, you may not realize while you're in your well-heated bubble, but we're freezing. Literally."

"No," was all Miriam had to say. "Go back to your little beds and tuck yourselves in, nice and warm."

Antony gasped, "Did she just tell us to die? I think she just told us to go to eternal rest." Angus mouthed a confused "what the fuck" and Jessie bit her lip to withhold the laughter bubbling from her stomach.

Miriam, incredulous that such an icon of stupidity sat before her, took some steps down and bent over to his level. "I told you to get your little bottoms off my concrete, now, before I call Sans."

"Sans wouldn't hurt a fly," Antony challenged with some spit. "Bring it, Bickel. No sleep 'til we get some fuckin' heat!" Hyped up for his cause, he beat his chest like a stone-age warrior and clutched the poster board so hard that it wrinkled. Once Miriam left, either to retrieve their parents or call Sans, Jessie burst into laughter and Angus just stared at his insane partner-in-crime, half-bewildered and half-bemused.

Gerard was the first to come down. It was the morning after for him, and he wasn't quite in the mood for his son's enthusiasm. "I understand and respect your cause," he stated before Antony could start pleading, "but there must be a more efficient way. We'll think of something. Upstairs, where it's a little less chilly."

COMPLEXES

"No way," Antony retorted. "I'm staying here. Damn efficiency. We're getting it done my way, I swear that to you."

James arrived to a scene of bickering Shepherds. "Angus," he said in a voice that was difficult to decipher, "what are you doing?" Standing his ground, Angus explained as if he were an avid follower of the cause. James chewed on this information quietly before ultimately sitting down behind Angus, arms and legs crossed, without another word. When Miriam and Marie arrived, he decisively stated, "I stand by my son."

The Shepherds, who were arguing until now, were silenced by James's resolution. Only after giving his son the "I'm going to kill you later for this" look, Gerard, not to be out-classed by James, promptly collapsed his legs and sat down right where he had stood. Knowing his voice would carry much less strength than that of his nemesis, Gerard simply nodded (almost apologetically) to Miriam.

"This is ridiculous," Miriam spat out. "Get your daughter out of this mess."

Marie, who, like Jessie, found the entire situation hilarious, covered her mouth. "I'm sorry, Mrs. Bickel. The cold must be getting to them."

Miriam, like an ugly goddess forced to condescend to earthlings, sighed in defeat. "Must I explain myself to you? I can't heat more than two apartments per floor.

CHAPTER NINE

Otherwise the heat would break. Leave if you want to. Good luck finding a different apartment in this weather." She ascended the stairs, leaving the small crowd at the boiler room to think on her words.

"No sleep 'til heat!" yelled Antony a final time before his father knocked gently on the back of his head.

Jessie looked desperately at her mother, to James, to Gerard, the responsible parents of the motley crew. "Is there really nothing we can do?"

"Our contract states that we have built-in utilities," James finally said the obvious. "We could sue her. The entire building can sue her."

"Yeah, all we need is a lawyer and time," Gerard cut in, clearly not a fan of the suing idea. "Time we don't have, and money I can't spend. It's a pain enough to get groceries in this weather." His bones cracked as he stood up. "If you think it's worth it, let me know. Otherwise, we're going back upstairs." Antony gave a small protest before surrendering to his father's glare.

Angus inquired in a small voice, "Do you think it's worth it, Dad?"

James sighed and followed Gerard's lead in standing. "You kids started this cause," he said. "If you want to end it, just let me know. I'll lend a hand." With that, Angus and Jessie stood and followed the line up the stairs.

COMPLEXES

The boiler room was at peace, but Antony, of course, would find another way.

A day after the Speare tea party and Jonathan saw no change. Giles did ask if he had a hand in arranging the encounter, but apart from that, he gave no indication that the event even took place. They went on living awkwardly around each other, sometimes jabbing at one another with double meanings and dares. Lingering in Jonathan's mind was the raw fact that his time with Giles was almost over. Sure, they'd be neighbors, but the intimacy they once shared had become a glass between them, slowly darkening to opaque.

Jonathan had just returned from purchasing last-minute provisions and obligatory art supplies to hoard while they spent their early winter confined when he saw the first few bits of Giles's clothing packed. A few T-shirts and jeans tucked inside a duffel bag couldn't have hurt him more. Half-tempted to call Giles out on his passive-aggressive moving habits, Jonathan tried to focus more on organizing his messy room, on rationing percentages of food for each day, and on searching for inspiration to dampen his dry spell while trapped in the Complexes. With each thought he became progressively more frustrated. Giles

CHAPTER NINE

invaded his mind, sitting on his neurons cross-legged with a nonchalant smile. He wanted to punch him.

"Giles," Jonathan called.

"What?" the voice came from the bathroom. Following it, the sound of water spraying from the showerhead. Jonathan mentally groaned at the timing of Giles's shower. But if there was any moment to catch a guy vulnerable, it was now.

Jonathan knocked on the bathroom door. "Can we talk?"

"It's unlocked."

One hand on the doorknob, the other fist clenched purposefully, Jonathan entered. Though Giles's clothes were strewn on the toilet seat, many of his toiletries were tucked away in a little bag on the sink—even his toothbrush. "Is this your last day here?" he asked, not masking the anger in his voice.

"Where?"

He knew full well "where," and was, once again, toying around with vulnerabilities in conversation. "You know what I mean," Jonathan said, choosing not to play his games.

"Here on earth?" Giles commenced listing the possibilities. "Here in the Complexes, here with you? Pick." As always, he liked to pinpoint Jonathan's pressure points. As always, he somehow managed to make Jonathan feel silly admitting the obvious.

COMPLEXES

Once again refusing, he chose none of the above. "You know," he repeated.

His silhouette behind the shower curtain, before moving, now stood still. Jonathan, knowing he would lose his resolve, looked away, instead focusing on the white tiled walls. "Yes," Giles said, "I do know. But I want to hear you say it."

"Say what?" Jonathan regretted the words, knowing he had played straight into Giles's hands.

"The truth."

"Truth is," he responded, voice laced with heated spite, "you're running away."

Giles's silence led Jonathan to believe that he had succeeded in a round of his games. But then he rebounded. "That could be true. But it isn't quite yet."

Furious, he pressed on, fingers pointing. "I have evidence. Exhibit A: the duffel bag by your side of the bed half-filled with clothes. Exhibit B: your toothbrush in that stupid girly makeup bag."

"I happen to be showering, not running. Jury's still out on that particular truth."

"If you're not running away, then my hair is the color of the sea." Giles's responding laugh did not do well to quell Jonathan's nerves. Unable to conjure up more clever comebacks and conclusions, he spat out, "Fuck you, Giles."

CHAPTER NINE

"Oh?" His silhouette turned, amused by the sudden change in banter. "What did you come here for, anyway?"

Unsure of his answer, Jonathan spewed out insults like a hose on jet settings. "Just to tell you you're full of bullshit, your haircut looks stupid, and to possibly punch you in the face."

In a tone of mild disappointment, Giles ignored the threat. "That wasn't what I was referring to. Now, what did you come here for, anyway?"

Repeating himself would do no good, but Jonathan had no idea what Giles was getting at. Essentially, he'd come to tell him how hurt he felt at his leaving. Now, duty done, he ought to leave, and let leave. But Giles's question, he knew, would gnaw at him through even the deepest dreams. What had he come here for?

"Here on earth, here in the Complexes, here with you. Pick."

And then he knew, he knew from the very beginning what he wanted. Somewhere in the middle, what he wanted had turned into so much more.

"I came here to be with you."

The shower water was cold—had been cold for days—but Jonathan didn't care. He pulled aside the curtain to see Giles, who was waiting for him as if he knew—and of course he knew all along—that Jonathan would kiss him and tell him he loved him and that if he was full of shit he was the most beautiful piece of shit. And

COMPLEXES

Giles, vulnerable in his arms, kissed him back.

During their first family meal together, breakfast, Angus didn't quite know how to feel. Remembering Jessie and her constant anxiety, he summed up his emotions and labeled the jar "nervous," because that's what people are when they have something to lose. Mara quietly finished cooking the scrambled eggs at the stove; James drank his coffee while staring at an unopened newspaper, leg bopping up and down. Giles emerged from his just reclaimed room and sat down on his old, designated side of the table, his old mug steaming with mocha. And Angus—he just wanted to take in the scene.

"What are you staring at?" Mara commented with a smile. If she was nervous, she hid it well. When she told Angus earlier that Giles was coming home for breakfast, she said, "Everyone has to stick together. That means we all put an effort in. Okay?"

Angus had agreed, but it was easier said than done. Upon sitting down, his first impulse was to take his phone out of his pocket and shoot Jessie a good morning text. With a wary look to his father, he decided against it. There. Putting effort in.

CHAPTER NINE

After the eggs finished cooking, Mara placed the final plate on the table and sat down. They sipped quietly on their respective drinks, but no one bit the fresh bait.

"I hear," Giles said, "that people are evacuating the city."

"Where'd you hear that? Doesn't say a word about it here." James put the newspaper down.

He shrugged. "Some college friends. Some people on our floor have already left."

Concerned, Angus piped in, "Should we leave?"

James grunted in response. "Leave it to the eccentric college kids to make it an apocalypse. It's just a bad freeze." Still, they shivered in their jackets layered over sweaters.

Morbidly, Giles persisted, "It's going to be too cold to stay in an unheated room."

"Should we sue?" Angus once again questioned.

"It's up to you." James sighed. "If you ask me, it's already too late."

"Sue?" Giles looked amused at the concept. To that, Angus explained the double sit-in situation in the boiler room. The first time, they gave up because there were more important things on their minds. The second time, well, they gave Miriam a scare, but nothing could be done. "Is our building that screwed up?" Giles laughed.

It was refreshing to hear, like a peal of bells after a church's closing. Angus smiled to himself. Despite the fact that the laughter was over irony on an almost apocalyptic scale, he didn't mind. It was his brother, looking content even in the presence of his family. If that wasn't an accomplishment, Angus didn't know what else was.

Over dishes, one on drying and one on rinsing, Angus apologized to Giles. "I was being angry and immature," he said. When they looked at each other across the hot steam rising from the sink, they knew that they both cared, but each wanted to see who would be the first to break the ice that separated them. They knew that whoever cared least appeared stronger. And they knew that that logic simply rendered them pitifully alone.

"So," Giles said after graciously accepting the apology, "I hear you have a girlfriend?"

Angus reddened. "She's not really my girlfriend." More absentmindedly, he wondered, what, exactly they were. Nowadays, they talked on a regular basis. He informed her of certain aspects of family drama; he felt it was right since she nearly spilled her own heart out in a river. They kissed that one time; it was as platonic as kissing could get, but it left a tingling on his mouth that urged for more. Jessie drew him in with her nervous mystique and spunky style. If only she could be his girlfriend.

CHAPTER NINE

"Is it the girl next door?" Giles persisted.

"She's not that type." Then, flushing after realizing what Giles really meant, he confirmed his suspicions. "Jessie. Asian, petite, has short hair." His brother paused in his rinsing, considering his newfound information. Angus opened and closed his mouth, wondering how to convey Jessie's story without tattling. "She has depression." He finally settled on upfront diagnosis. At Giles's curious look, Angus covered his steps, saying, "I'm telling you because I don't really know how to deal with it."

Giles frowned. "She's dealing with it, not you."

"But, you know what I mean."

A little more forcefully, Giles continued, "If she's got that weight on her shoulders, she has to put it down and sort it all out. You can hold her hand, but you can't touch the materials, even if she tries to hand them to you." His eyes narrowed slightly, as if looking deeper into himself than into the dishwashing set before him. "I'm not saying broken people don't make good partners. I'm saying that fixers don't."

Knowing by his brother's tone that he was finished talking, Angus remained pensive for the remainder of the chore. Leave it to his brother to speak in strange analogies. Leave it to his brother to make perfect sense.

After dishes, after the family dispersed, Angus paced in his room, waiting

COMPLEXES

for a reasonable hour to knock on Jessie's door. Once the clock struck eleven—most restaurants and stores are open by eleven, right?—he went to her. His hand felt heavy at his side as he raised it to knock. The always hospitable Marie answered the door.

Breathless and shaking, he politely asked for Jessie. With a knowing look, Marie called Jessie to the door and courteously left the two to discuss. Wearing a giant hoodie and no makeup, she shot him a quizzical look. Angus still couldn't shake the awe and fright that sunk into his stomach upon seeing her.

"I'll wait for you."

"What?"

Angus swallowed, and delved into a mix of what he had planned on saying and what he desperately needed to say. "I'll wait for you, until you get better, until you're ready, until you feel up to having a boyfriend like me around. I've made myself clear that I like you—and I really like you—and I know you're hesitant because—because of reasons—but point is, I'll wait for you."

Jessie's face softened. With a loose hand at the center of her chest, she responded as if relaying information from the heart, "I'm really touched, really. And I do like you too, Angus. But I'm still scared that I'll never get better, that I'll never be good enough for you, or that you'll end up just leaving. I don't want to lose you, too."

CHAPTER NINE

Angus, undone by her response, stammered. There was more he wanted to say to her—anything to stop that sinking in her eyes. But that was what Giles was talking about when he said "fixer," wasn't it? Luckily enough, Jessie read his confusion and allowed him time to bring his thoughts up through his throat. "I'll wait for you," he repeated, third time's the charm. "Even if things don't get better, I'd like to think I'll always be there for you. Maybe someday you'll learn to love yourself—and then give me time to learn to love you."

The hand at Jessie's chest rose to her face. "Angus, I'm sorry," she quietly wept, "I'm a box of doubt, and I want more than anything to be your girlfriend instead. I'm sorry for making you wait."

"You're not making me do anything, silly," Angus said. He held open his arms. "I'm here if you need me."

When she entered into his arm span, they didn't become one. They became two, holding each other tight, crying over what seemed like a farfetched promise. But all they wanted was happiness for the other—if it meant waiting, asking for platonic kisses, asking for a crutch to lean on while wounds healed, they would settle for this selfless, unromantic   conclusion.

COMPLEXES

Chapter Ten

The idea spawned from Morrissey's kindness and Ruthy's casual indifference. Then it caught on like wildfire, opening doors like smashes of wind. Antony and Morrissey knocked on the doors of the occupied rooms, greeted whoever it was with a smile, and invited them to their cozy, heated abode for the day. "It's 'bring your own beer'—or food or whatever," Antony said, "But we'll exchange heat for some good company."

Jonathan and his regular visitor Giles were the first to wholeheartedly accept. With a battered old laptop that could play old DVDs, they watched movies on Ruthy's couch. Sometimes when they thought Antony wasn't looking they'd display their lover's affections with a discreet kiss. Morrissey was thrilled to have college kids in her presence, and liked to sporadically interrupt their movie with questions and her strange speculations. They entertained her, gladly treating her as if she were a young adult herself. Whatever she wondered, Giles wondered with her. "She's funny, that girl," Jonathan commented to Antony over tea. "Sometimes she's petty, but other times she's witty and downright deep." Otherwise, Giles and Jonathan preferred mostly to be left alone. Antony would have kept them company, had their long list of DVDs not been so slow-paced and overly bizarre.

Gerard kept a stiff spine whenever Giles was in the room; he was perceptibly unnerved by the young man and his way of talking in circles. When Antony asked why, he told his date-disaster story, thus leaving his son with the impression that Giles was happily heartless to his enemies.

Jonathan, on the other hand, seemed too normal for Giles. However, Antony observed that, unlike most people, Jonathan went beyond toleration of Giles's word games. He played them, chewed on them like a dog toy until he figured out how and why they squeaked. They'd banter over movie dialogues, arguing character development or something involved like that. "Can't you just be straightforward about things?" was Jonathan's one complaint. Giles shot him down with an ironic monosyllable.

Martha was the next to have the heat, and the next to open her doors. Early morning, everyone on floor E flocked to her apartment to partake in the warmth and to taste of her abundance of teas. She was overjoyed to have so many people to share teatime with, that each ounce of loose tea tethered into a little bag wasn't a waste to her. "Who else is going to drink all this?" she said when Antony voiced his concern.

Antony noticed Gerard's anxious behavior once Mara and James entered. James, who was cut off from work completely, was his same intimidating self, granted he looked a little softer around the edges, as if he actually breathed the same oxygen that Antony himself breathed. While he mostly remained quiet, reading, Mara was content to spark flames of conversation with just about anyone. During the coming weeks, Ruthy grew quite fond of her. "She's like a younger sister I never had," she said wistfully to Antony once. "I can understand why Gerard liked her so much. She has that maternal charm I never had. I can't imagine her not being a mother."

She and Gerard exchanged no words, mostly because Gerard was inclined to remain on the other side of the room from her. Mara didn't look in the least uncomfortable. Once, she asked Antony with concern how Gerard was doing. Squeezing his arm, she said with eyes that conveyed her condolences but not her regret, "I'm sorry." As much as Antony would have liked the two to talk, he accepted the apology on his father's behalf.

The Speare family of course was completed with Angus, who usually settled himself with Jessie, Antony, and Morrissey around a table, discussing things that varied from social justice to their pet peeve fashion trends. "Clogs are the weirdest fashion statement. It's like—hey, feet are super ugly so let's make stuff that make them look super ugly!"

CHAPTER TEN

Jessie, a proud clog-wearer herself, countered Angus's statement. "Clogs are so comfortable. And they're cute when they're in plaid—ooh, or suede. In short, your argument sucks balls."

When they ran out of things to say (which typically happened during long afternoons or in the mornings when they were too tired), they entertained themselves with board games and cards. Morrissey refused to play Monopoly against Antony—for good reason—for he was far to conniving and lucky, and landed on Free Parking whenever the center of the board was chock-full of cash. He won five games in a row, thus forcing Morrissey and Jessie to either ban Monopoly from the Complexes or ban Antony from Monopoly.

Antony invited his father to play or talk; he refrained despite his looking listless. Figuring that his father refused to be on board with a Speare because their presences felt like a one to the throat, Antony left him alone.

Gerard did spend a lot of time with Ruthy, tracing over journeys across the country and reminiscing on good days of the past when Gerard wasn't hooked on drugs or off with Alice. "How is the old man doing?" he asked quietly one night, when he thought Antony was asleep.

"He's old, tired, not really thinking of you," Ruthy responded tactlessly. "Like I said, you broke their hearts and their wallets, but they patched themselves right up." In a lower voice, she added, "They ask a lot about Morrissey. Always, 'Oh, our only grandchild!' I've told them about Antony, but they pretend like he doesn't exist."

Nightly talks like these, with everyone asleep on blow-up mattresses or sleeping bags, had Antony eavesdropping left and right. One particularly interesting conversation was between Giles, Mara, and James. Had Angus been awake, he'd have turned red in mortification and fury.

It began with, "How are things between you two?" and swooped downhill as Giles grew more and more aggressive with his curiosity. Unabashed as always, he asked, "So are you two having sex again?"

When Giles did decide to be straightforward, man, he did not beat around the bush. Mara covered her mouth to hide a laugh. James made that strained face he always made when he was struggling to understand his sons. When he did not get a satisfactory answer, Giles justified himself, saying, "I'm curious if sex gets better or worse with age. Is it like drugs, where you're searching for that first astonishing orgasm? Or—"

"Stop it, Giles." Mara giggled, flushed. "Yes, we've been intimate." She looked to James, who seemed in disbelief that this conversation was actually happening.

Miriam hardly noticed the cooperative "cheating the system." Sans noticed, often joined on his breaks, but never mentioned it to her. When she did, it was far too inhumane, even for her, to protest. Floor E continued this newfound tradition, facing the soon to be month-long blizzard without much concern for the cold. "Are you happy we stayed?" Gerard asked not selfishly on the fifth day before Antony trotted off to meet with his friends.

At that, he simply smiled. "When does my goofy grin mean anything other than happiness?"

The storm had no mercy the morning after Ruthy's death. It happened in E02, probably in the morning. Her body was cold when Gerard tried to wake her up. Everyone on floor E witnessed his desperation as he searched for a pulse to tell him that she was still alive, croaky-throated and all. Jessie ran out of the room to hide tears she felt were invasive. Antony stopped his father from shaking the corpse, holding him like a crying child. Morrissey was silent.

The ambulance's arrival was delayed, so they placed her in her icy bed, folded her hands in stony prayer. Gerard's tears stopped flowing, his expression replaced with one of emotional exhaustion. Antony stared out the window, as if trying to trace the leftovers of her soul's ascent to heaven. No DVDs were played. Everyone spoke in low whispers.

COMPLEXES

When her body was taken, it was to be held in a morgue until the blizzard calmed. The EMTs, who were in the process covering Ruthy with a sheet, did not wince when Morrissey kicked the wall and slapped at the body like a windmill. "Stupid!" she screamed. "This is so–goddamn–stupid!"

Gerard held her back as the body was moved. Though her cheeks were red and she panted heavily, she seemed to have nothing else to say, and retreated back into her shell. A dark curtain covered her blue eyes.

Ruthy's will was saved as a document on an old, mostly unused laptop. Naturally, everything Ruthy owned went to Morrissey. Morrissey was to go live with her grandparents in California. "She can't go there now," Gerard protested over the phone to the official, clearly perplexed that his dear sister hadn't entrusted her daughter, her treasure, to him. In this weather, few flights, if any, left the airport. "I'll take care of her. Then I'll bring her to her grandparents."

Antony, of course, listened in. Once his father hung up, his face looked sunken with worry. "We're going back to California?"

"I can't send Morrissey to my parents and then never see her again." Gerard could do nothing to lift the disappointment off his son's shoulders. "Without Ruthy's help, we can't stay here any longer."

CHAPTER TEN

Antony responded, more challenging than relenting, "Do you really think this storm is going to let up? Dad, Ruthy's gone, and we can't even dig deep enough to bury her underground. It's getting colder and colder every day, and soon enough no one can pay the rent because no one's gone to work."

"Don't tell me you believe in this apocalyptic bull that the television spews."

"Let's make a deal," Antony said, the fire igniting in his eyes warming the rest of his aura. "Once we can bury Ruthy, I'll go."

Gerard, perceiving this as surrender, accepted. Of course, how would he know that this time, the storm would not calm?

In the meantime, Morrissey covered herself in a blanket fort, with Ruthy's old laptop. She mumbled in her sleep and ignored the other two mothers on floor E who insisted on becoming temporary maternal figures. Whenever she could, she braved the cold and sat in the hallway with her mountain of fleece, whispering to herself as she typed.

Ever since James told her, it had boiled in her stomach. This matter had nothing to do with her, but, it might change two men's lives. With this information searing in her hands like a hot potato, she was always wary around Gerard, who was clearly avoiding her. She needed a good opportunity to speak to him—she figured, rude as it was, Ruthy's death gave her that opportunity.

As the heat switched from one room to another, she caught him rationing his food out for the week inside his chilly apartment. He was searching for the expiration date on a ramen noodle cup when she interrupted with a knock on the wall. "Gerard," she said, noting the awkwardness in the room become palpable with every condensing exhale, "can I speak with you?" Gerard stammered, but, not wanting to be rude, he nodded. Steeling herself, Mara began, "I'm so, so sorry for your loss. Ruthy was a wonderful woman. I was lucky to have squeezed in some time with her before she passed."

"Thanks," he said, voice dry in both meanings of the word. His attention returned back to the microwavable ramen cup.

Wringing her hands, Mara resumed. "There's something else I've been meaning to tell you." She fumbled with her words a bit, wondering how to keep his attention without being inconsiderate. "You see, James did cheat on me. He met a woman online, fell in love, and moved to the city to meet her. The relationship was one-sided because she didn't want to break up a family." Gerard looked at her expectantly. "That woman told my husband to man up and go back to his family, to tell them he

CHAPTER TEN

loves them. And because of her—because of Alice Bradshaw—I still have a family."

The name was, without doubt, all too familiar to Gerard. The hand that held the distracting cup of ramen trembled. "Alice," he said, the feel of the word heavy on his tongue.

Knowing he needed time to emotionally recuperate, Mara handed him a slip of paper with Alice's number written on it. The paper looked as though it could slip right through Gerard's fingertips. Message passed, Mara would have pushed from her head all responsibility over the tumultuous life of Gerard Shepherd had he not looked at her with mixed feelings of despair and genuine appreciation and said, "Thank you."

Antony huddled in a secondhand winter coat. For the first time in two weeks, he was completely alone. The college-ruled slip of paper in his hand felt heavy, as if it were drenched in the very wet of secrets. "It's your mother," Gerard had told him when he gave the paper away, like a gift never to be seen again.

"You don't want to talk to her first?"

Gerard shook his head and smiled, weakly. "I don't think I can face her."

All this time, she was in this city, so elusively close. And yet all this time, Gerard was too busy looking at another woman. Antony sadly laughed at the irony.

COMPLEXES

He wondered what he would say to a woman he considered dead. He wondered why it mattered what he said if he truly considered her dead. Inexplicably, his heart beat faster as every minute passed. If he stayed sitting here any longer, he figured he might have a heart attack like Ruthy.

No details were given to him except for Gerard's three-word statement. Antony daren't ask why she'd left—he found deep inside him this yearning to know so much more. Did she really brush her teeth every evening or did she accidentally forget some nights when she was too tired? Was she a West Coast person or an East Coast person? How did she usually wear her hair: long or short, blonde or not? Were her eyelashes long enough to tickle another person's cheek if she got close enough?

Suddenly, he felt a little like Morrissey.

Antony picked up the phone and dialed the number, referencing the note even though he had probably memorized it by now. The line rang its steely ring. If he breathed any louder he might wake the entire Complexes.

"Hello?" Her voice was calm, albeit a bit confused, as anyone would be if called by a random number. Antony felt as if someone had shoved a dry rock in his throat. He held his breath, afraid to move, afraid to make a sound. "Hello?" she repeated, holding out the "o" in a tiny singsong, gentle as a lullaby from seventeen years ago.

"Hi, Mom."

He had never looked for her, but now that he had found her, he never wanted to let go.

❄❄❄❄❄

"What are you writing?" A man sat beside her, a man she only knew by his last name, his scary face, and his reputation. Morrissey knew better than to ignore him like she had ignored everyone else. His appearance caused her to lose her train of thought; her fingers paused on the keyboard.

"A story," she answered tersely.

He replied, as if practicing conversation, "About what?"

Spreading her hands on the keyboard to feel the bumpy keys on her palm, she considered this. "People. Stupid people."

The man named Mr. Speare persisted. "What makes them stupid?"

With frustrated passion, she said, "They're stupid because they don't talk. They love each other—everyone loves each other, but they don't talk. So in the end, it all goes to shit. *Kaboom*." She used jazz hands for effect.

Mr. Speare asked, a little ashamed to play the question game, "Why don't they talk, though?"

264

COMPLEXES

"That," Morrissey confirmed, "is the ultimate question."

They pondered this as what was left of the sun trickled in through the hallway windows, through the venetian blinds, appearing like dusty stairways to heaven on the floor. The quiet whirring in the designated communal room died down, and all that was left was the sound of soft voices. As temperatures lowered and jackets flew onto shoulders, they shivered. The heat was broken, but outside, the world was wonderfully white.